The Young Explorer

By
Horatio Alger

CHAPTER I.

BEN'S INHERITANCE.

"I've settled up your father's estate, Benjamin," said Job Stanton. "You'll find it all figgered out on this piece of paper. There was that two-acre piece up at Rockville brought seventy-five dollars, the medder fetched a hundred and fifty, the two cows—"

"How much does it all come to, Uncle Job?" interrupted Ben, who was impatient of details.

"Hadn't you better let me read off the items, nephew?" asked Job, looking over his spectacles.

"No, Uncle Job. I know you've done your best for me, and there's no need of your going through it all. How much is there left after all expenses are paid?"

"That's what I was a-comin' to, Ben. I make it out that there's three hundred and sixty-five dollars and nineteen cents. That's a dollar for every day in the year. It's a good deal of money, Ben."

"So it is, Uncle Job," answered Ben, and he was quite sincere. There are not many boys of sixteen to whom this would not seem a large sum.

"You're rich; that is, for a boy," added Uncle Job.

"It's more than I expected, uncle. I want you to take fifteen dollars and nineteen cents. That'll leave me just three hundred and fifty."

"Why should I take any of your money, nephew?"

"You've had considerable trouble in settling up the estate, and it's taken a good deal of your time, too."

"My time ain't of much vally, and as to the trouble, it's a pity ef I can't take some trouble for my brother's son. No, Ben, I won't take a cent. You'll need it all."

"But you said yourself it was a good deal of money for a boy, Uncle

Job."

"So it is, but it's all you've got. Most boys have fathers to take care of 'em, while you're alone in the world."

"Yes I am alone in the world," said Ben sadly, his cheerful face clouding over.

"But you've got an uncle, lad," continued Job Stanton, laying his hand gently on the boy's shoulder. "He's a poor man, but as much as in him lies, he'll be your friend and helper."

"I know it, Uncle Job. You've always been kind to me."

"And allus will be, Ben. Now, Ben, I've got a plan for you. I don't know what you'll think of it, but it's the best I've been able to think of."

"What is it, Uncle Job?"

"Ef you'll stay with me and help me in the shop, I'll give you a home, such as it is, and fifty dollars a year toward your clothes. Your Aunt Hannah and your Cousin Jane want you to make your home with us."

"I'm very much obliged to you, Uncle Job," said Ben slowly.

"You needn't be, boy. It's a sort of mutooal arrangement. It'll be as good for me as for you. You can put your money in the bank, and let it stay till you're twenty-one. Why, it'll be nigh on to five hunderd dollars by that time."

"I'm much obliged to you, Uncle Job, as I said before, but there's one thing in the way."

"What's that, Ben?"

"I don't like shoemaking."

"Perhaps it isn't genteel enough for you, Ben," said his uncle.

"I don't care for that, Uncle Job, but I don't like being shut up in a shop. Besides, it doesn't give steady work. Last year you were without work at least a third of the time."

"So I was, Ben," said Job. "I'm willin' to own that's a great drawback."

"And it isn't likely to be any better hereafter. Last year was as good as the average."

"It was better," Job admitted. "The year before I was out of work five months."

"Well, Uncle Job, I want to work at something that'll give me employment all the year round."

"So do I, Ben, but I don't see what you can find, unless you go to work on a farm. You're used to that, and I guess you could find a chance before long. There's Deacon Pitkin wants a boy, and would be glad of the chance of gettin' you."

"I suppose he would," said Ben, laughing. "Would you advise me to go there?"

"Well, there might be some objections, but-"

"You know I wouldn't get enough to eat, Uncle Job," interrupted

Ben. "Why, Deacon Pitkin's the meanest man in the village."

"You mustn't be hasty in your judgments, nephew."

"I'm not. I know what I'm talking about. I worked for the deacon two days once. He gave me ten cents a day and board-and such board! Why, I got up from the table hungry every meal, and yet the deacon reported afterward that I was a great eater. Mrs. Pitkin cuts a small pie into eight pieces, each about two mouthfuls, and when I asked for a second piece, she asked if I was allowed to have two pieces at home."

"What did you say?" asked Uncle Job, evidently amused.

"I said yes, and that each piece was twice as big as she gave."

"I'm afraid that was rather forward, Ben. Did she say anything to that?"

"She said I must be very greedy, and that boys always ate more'n was good for 'em. No, Uncle Job, I don't care to work for Deacon Pitkin."

"Have you formed any plans, Ben? You don't want to go on a farm, and you don't want to go into a shoeshop, and that's about all you can find to do in Hampton."

"I don't mean to stay in Hampton," said Ben quietly.

"Don't mean to stay in Hampton!" exclaimed Uncle Joe, amazed.

"No, uncle. There's a good many places besides Hampton in the world."

"So there is, Ben," answered Uncle Job, with a disregard of grammar more excusable than his nephew's, for he had never had any special educational advantages,-"so there is, but you don't know anybody in them other places."

"It won't take me long to get acquainted," returned Ben, not at all disturbed by this consideration.

"Where do you want to go?"

"I want to go to California."

"Gracious sakes! Want to go to California!" gasped Job. "What put that idee into your head?"

"A good many people are going there, and there's a chance to get rich quick out among the gold-mines."

"But you're only a boy."

"I'm a pretty large boy, Uncle Job," said Ben complacently, "and I'm pretty strong."

"So you be, Ben, but it takes more than strength."

"What more, Uncle Job?"

"It takes judgment."

"Can't a boy have judgment?"

"Waal, he may have some, but you don't often find an old head on young shoulders."

"I know all that, uncle, but I can work if I am a boy."

"I know you're willin' to work, Ben, but it'll cost a sight of money to get out to Californy to start with."

"I know that. It will take two hundred dollars."

"And that's more'n half of all you've got. It seems to me temptin' Providence to spend such a sight of money for the chance of earning some on t'other side of the world, when you can get a livin' here and put all your money in the bank."

"In five years it would only amount to five hundred dollars, and if I go to California, I expect to be worth a good deal more than that before two years are past."

"I'm afraid you've got large idees, Ben."

"You won't interfere with my going, Uncle Job?" asked Ben anxiously.

"I won't actooly interfere, but I'll do all I can to have you give it up."

"But if my mind is set upon it, you'll let me go, won't you, uncle?"

"I suppose I must," said Job Stanton. "A wilful lad must have his way. But you mustn't blame me if things turn out unlucky."

"No, I shall only blame myself."

"There's one promise you must make me," said his uncle.

"What is that?"

"Take a week to consider whether you hadn't better take my advice and stay at home."

"Yes, uncle, I'll promise that."

"And you'll think it over in all its bearin's?"

"Yes, uncle."

"It ain't best to take any important step without reflection, Ben."

"You're right, uncle."

This conversation took place in Job Stanton's little shoe-shop, only a rod distant from the small, plain house which he had occupied ever since he had been married. It was interrupted by the appearance of a pretty girl of fourteen, who, presenting herself at the door of the shop, called out:

"Supper's ready, father."

"So are we, Jennie," said Ben, promptly.

"You are always ready to eat, Ben," said his cousin, smiling.

"That's what Mrs. Pitkin used to think, Jennie. She used to watch every mouthful I took."

CHAPTER II.

DEACON PITKIN'S OFFER.

Ben's father had died three months before. He had lost his mother when ten years old, and having neither brother nor sister was left quite alone in the world. At one time his father had possessed a few thousand dollars, but by unlucky investments he had lost nearly all, so that Ben's inheritance amounted to less than four hundred dollars.

This thought troubled Mr. Stanton, and on his death-bed he spoke about it to his son.

"I shall leave you almost destitute, Ben," he said. "If I had acted more wisely it would have been different."

"Don't trouble yourself about that, father," said Ben promptly. "I am young and strong, and I shall be sure to get along."

"You will have to work hard, and the world is a hard taskmaster."

"I don't feel afraid, father. I am sure I shall succeed."

The dying father was cheered by Ben's confident words. Our hero was strong and sturdy, his limbs active, and his face ruddy with health. He looked like a boy who could get along. He was not a sensitive plant, and not to be discouraged by rebuffs. The father's brow cleared.

"I am glad you are not afraid to meet what is in store for you," he said. "I believe you will do your part, and God helps those who help themselves."

After his father's death, Ben became an inmate of his uncle's family while the estate was being settled. He paid for his board partly by work in the shop, and partly by doing chores. This brings us to the day when the conversation detailed in the first chapter took place.

On the following morning Ben was sent on an errand to the village store. On his way he overtook Deacon Pitkin.

"Good mornin', Ben!" said the deacon. "Where are you goin'?"

"To the store, sir."

"So am I. Ef you ain't in a hurry, le'ss walk along together."

"All right, sir," answered Ben. "I think I know what's comin," he said to himself.

"You're stayin' at your Uncle Job's, ain't you?" asked Deacon

Pitkin.

"Yes, sir."

"You don't calc'late to keep on there, do you?"

"No, sir; he would like to have me stay and work in the shop, but I don't fancy shoemaking."

"Jest so. I wouldn't ef I was you. It's an onsartin business.

There's nothin' like farmin' for stiddy work."

"The old man kept me at work pretty stiddy," thought Ben. "He'd always find something for me to do."

"'Ive been thinkin' that I need a boy about your age to help me on my farm. I ain't so young as I was, and I've got a crick in my back. I don't want a man-"

"You'd have to pay him too high wages," Ben said to himself.

"A strong, capable boy like you could give me all the help I need."

"I expect I could," said Ben demurely.

"I was sayin' to Mrs. Pitkin this mornin' that I thought it would be a good plan to take you till you was twenty-one."

"What did she say?" asked Ben, interested.

"Waal, she didn't say much," answered the deacon slowly; "but I guess she hasn't no objections."

"Didn't she say that I had an awful appetite?" asked Ben, smiling.

"She said you was pretty hearty," answered the deacon, rather surprised at Ben's penetration. "Boys should curb their appetites."

"I don't think I could curb mine," said Ben thoughtfully.

"I guess there wouldn't be any trouble about that," returned the deacon, whose meanness ran in a different channel from his wife's, and who took less note of what was eaten at his table. "Ef you think you'd like to engage, and we could make a bargain, you might begin next week."

"Jest so," said Ben.

The deacon looked at him rather sharply, but Ben didn't appear to intend any disrespect in repeating his favorite phrase.

"Did your father leave you much?" inquired Deacon Pitkin.

"A few hundred dollars," said Ben carelessly.

"Indeed!" said the deacon, gratified. "What are you goin' to do with it?"

"Uncle Job thinks it would be best to put it in the bank."

"Jest so. It would fetch you some interest every year-enough to clothe you, likely. I'll tell you what I'll do, Ben. I'll give you your board the first year, and your interest will buy your clothes. The second year I'll give you twenty dollars and board, and maybe twenty more the third year."

Ben shook his head.

"I guess we can't make a bargain, Deacon Pitkin," he said.

Deacon Pitkin knew that he had made a very mean offer, and felt that he could afford to increase it somewhat; but he was a close hand at a bargain, and meant to get Ben as cheap as he could.

"What was you expectin'?" he asked cautiously. "You must remember that you're only a boy, and can't expect men's wages."

Ben had no idea, as we know, of engaging to work for Deacon Pitkin at all; but he decided that the easiest way to avoid it was to put such a value on his services as to frighten the old man.

"I am almost as strong as a man," he said, "and I can earn a great deal more than my board the first year."

"I might be willin' to give you twenty dollars the first year," said the deacon.

"I've been thinking," said Ben soberly, "that I ought to have a hundred and fifty dollars and board the first year."

Deacon Pitkin fairly gasped for breath. He was fairly overpowered by
Ben's audacity.

"A-hundred-and-fifty-dollars!" he ejaculated, turning his wrinkled face toward
our hero.

"That's about the figure," said Ben cheerfully. "A hundred and fifty dollars and
board, or three hundred dollars, and I'll board with my uncle."

"Is the boy crazy?" asked the deacon, in a bewildered tone.

"You'd have to pay a man as much as twenty dollars a month," pursued
Ben. "That's about a hundred dollars a year more."

"Benjamin," said the deacon solemnly, "do you want to ruin me?"

"No, sir, I hope not," answered our hero innocently.

"Then why do you ask such an unheard-of price?"

"I think I'm worth it," said Ben.

"Boys haven't much jedgment," said the deacon. "You'd better let me talk over
this matter with your Uncle Job."

"It won't be any use, Deacon Pitkin. Uncle Job won't interfere with me."

"You can't get such wages anywhere. You'll have to work for less."

"Perhaps I can't get my price in Hampton," said Ben.

"Of course you can't. There ain't no one goin' to pay you men's wages."

"Perhaps you are right, Deacon Pitkin. In that case, my mind is made up."

"What will you do?" asked the deacon, showing some curiosity.

"I'll leave town."

"It's a resky thing, Benjamin. You ain't old enough to take care of yourself."

"I think I can do it. Deacon Pitkin. I am not afraid to try. Still, if you'll give me
a hundred and fifty dollars and board—"

"You must think I'm crazy," said the deacon hastily. "I don't throw money
away that way."

"Then I'm afraid we can't make a bargain, deacon. Here is the store, and I'll bid
you good morning."

"If you think better of my offer, you can let me know, Benjamin. You can talk
it over with your uncle."

"All right, sir. If you think better of mine, just let me know within a week, or I
may be gone from Hampton."

"That's a cur'us boy," said the deacon meditatively. "He's got the most conceited idea of his vally to work of any boy I ever came across. A hundred and fifty dollars and board! What'll Mrs. Pitkin say when I tell her? She ain't much sot on the boy's comin' anyway. She thinks he's too hearty; but I don't mind that, so much. He's strong and good to work, an' he's the only boy in town that would suit me."

"I wonder what the deacon thinks of me," soliloquized Ben. "I thought I should scare him a little when I named my price. If I'd thought he would take me at that figure, I'd have said more. It wouldn't suit me to work for him at all."

In the evening Deacon Pitkin came over to see Job Stanton, and renewed his offer for Ben's services.

"The boy's got wild idees about pay," he said; "but boys haven't much jedgment. You're a sensible man, Mr. Stanton, and you and me can make a fair bargain."

"It won't be of much use, Deacon Pitkin. Ben's got his idees, an' he sticks to 'em."

"But you're his uncle. You can make him see his true interest."

"Ben's young," said Job, suspending his work; "but he's got to look out for himself. He may make mistakes, but I've promised not to interfere. I've got confidence in him that he'll come out right in the end. Truth is, deacon, he don't want to work at farmin', and that's why he asked you such a steep price. He knew you wouldn't agree to give it."

This put the matter in a new light, and Deacon Pitkin reluctantly concluded that he must abandon the idea of obtaining Ben as a helper on his farm.

CHAPTER III.

SAM STURGIS' NEW IDEA.

During the week which Ben had agreed to take before coming to a final decision, he had another offer of employment.

This is how it came about:

A little out of the village, in a handsome house, the best in Hampton, lived Major Sturgis, a wealthy landholder, who had plenty to live upon and nothing in particular to do, except to look after his property. He was a portly man, who walked with a slow, dignified step, leaning on a gold-headed cane, and evidently felt his importance. His son, Sam, was a chip of the old block. He condescended to associate with the village boys, because solitary grandeur is not altogether pleasant. He occasionally went to New York to visit a cousin of about his own age. From such a visit he had just returned, bringing back with him a new idea.

"Father," he said, "Cousin Henry has a boy about his own age to wait on him, black his boots, and run errands."

"Has he?" asked the major mechanically, not looking up from the daily paper which he was reading.

"Yes, sir. He don't pay him much, you know, only five dollars a month and his board, and Henry finds it very convenient."

Major Sturgis did not reply. In fact, he was too much interested in the article he was reading.

"Ain't you as rich as uncle?" asked Sam, who was gradually leading up to his proposal.

"Yes, Sam, I think so," answered his father, laying down the paper and removing his gold-bowed spectacles.

"Then why won't you let me have a servant, too?"

"What do you want of a servant? There are servants enough in the house."

"I want a boy to follow me round, and do just what I bid him."

"I don't see any necessity for it."

"He could do errands for you, too, father," said Sam diplomatically.

"We would have to send to the city for a boy, in case I let you have one."

"No, we wouldn't," answered Sam.

"Do you know of any one around here?"

"Yes; there is Ben Stanton. He's got to find something to do."

"I thought you didn't like Ben Stanton," said the major, in some surprise. "I have heard you say-"

"Oh, he's rather uppish-feels too big for a poor boy; but I would soon train him. I'd make him know his place."

"Your remarks are well founded, my son. Only yesterday I met the boy on the village street, and instead of taking off his hat and making a low bow, as he should do to a man of my position, he nodded carelessly, and said. 'How are you, major?' Really, I don't know what the country is coming to, when the rising generation is so deficient in veneration."

"The fact is, father, Ben thinks himself as good as anybody. You'd think, by the way he speaks to me, that he considered himself my equal."

"That is one of the evils incident to a republican form of government," said the major pompously. "For my part, I prefer the English social system, where the gentry are treated with proper deference."

"Well, father, may I engage Ben as my servant?"

"I am afraid you would not find him properly subordinate."

"Just leave that to me," said Sam confidently. "If I can't teach him his place, then nobody can. I should enjoy having him to order about."

Sam generally carried his point with his father, and the present instance was no exception.

"I don't know that I have any particular objection," said the major.

"How much wages may I offer, father?"

"The same that your Cousin Henry's servant gets."

"All right, sir," said Sam, with satisfaction. "I guess I'll go round, and see him about it this afternoon. I suppose he can come any time?"

"Yes, my son."

As Sam went out of the room his father thought, complacently:

"My son has all the pride and instincts of a gentleman. He will do credit to the family."

Few persons in the village would have agreed with the major. Sam Sturgis was decidedly unpopular. No boy who puts on airs is likely to be a favorite with any class of persons, and Sam put on rather more than he was entitled to. From time to time he received a rebuff, but still money will tell. He had his followers and sycophants, but we may be sure that Ben was not numbered among them. It was quite useless for Sam to patronize him-he would not be patronized, but persisted in treating the major's son with the most exasperating familiarity. Of course this would be impossible if he became Sam's servant, and this more than anything else was the motive of the young aristocrat in wishing to engage him. As to conferring a favor on Ben, that was the last thing in his thoughts.

Sam bent his steps toward the humble home of Job Stanton, but he did not have to go the whole distance. He met Ben with a fishing-pole over his shoulder.

"How are you, Sam?" was Ben's familiar greeting. "Want to go fishing with me?"

"He's entirely too familiar," thought Sam. "I'll cure him of that when he is under my orders."

At present Sam did not think it politic to express his feelings on the subject.

Ben was so independent that it might frustrate his plan.

"I will walk along with you, Ben," said Sam condescendingly.

"All right. Haven't you got a fishing-pole at home?"

"Yes, I have a very handsome one; it cost five dollars."

"Then it's rather ahead of mine," said Ben.

"I should say so," remarked Sam, surveying Ben's pole with contempt.

"But I'll bet you can't catch as many fish with it," said Ben promptly. "I don't think it makes much difference to the fish," he added, with a laugh, "whther they are caught with a five-dollar pole or a five-cent one."

"Very likely," said Sam briefly, "but I prefer to use a nice pole."

"Oh, there's no objection," said Ben, "if you fancy it. It doesn't make any difference to me."

"When are you going to work?" asked Sam abruptly.

"I am working every day-that is, I am helping Uncle Job."

"But I suppose you mean to get regular work somewhere, don't you?"

"What's he after, I wonder?" thought Ben. "Maybe I do," he said aloud.

"Perhaps I can throw something in your way," said Sam, in a patronizing way.

"You are very kind," said Ben, who supposed Sam had heard of some business position which he could fill. Our hero decided that perhaps he had misjudged the major's son, and he was prepared to make amends. "If you get me a position, I shall be much obliged."

"The fact is," said Sam, "I should find it convenient to have a boy go about with me, and be at my orders. My Cousin Henry has one, and father says I may engage you."

Ben faced round, and looked steadily at Sam. He felt that he would far rather work for Deacon Pitkin, in spite of his meager table, or toil twelve hours a day in his uncle's shoe-shop, than accept such a place as was now offered him. He penetrated Sam's motive, and felt incensed with him, though he did not choose to show it.

"What are you willing to pay?" asked Ben, in a businesslike tone.

"Five dollars a month and your board," said Sam. "You'll live better than you ever did before in your life, and your duties will be easy."

"What would you want me to do?" asked Ben.

"Why, I would take you with me whenever I went out rowing or fishing. That would be easy enough. Then, in the morning you would black my shoes and keep my clothes well brushed, and go of any errands I had for you. Oh, well, I can't tell you all you would have to do, but you'd have an easy time."

"Yes, I don't think it would tire me out," said Ben. "You'd want me to black your boots?"

"Yes."

"Well, I might agree to that on one condition."

"What is that?"

"That you would black mine."

"What do you mean?" demanded Sam, his face flushing angrily.

"Just what I say."

"Do you mean to insult me?"

"Not a bit; any more than you mean to insult me,"

"Do you dare to propose that I, a gentleman, should black your low-lived shoes?" exclaimed Sam furiously.

"I think you're rather hard on my shoes," said Ben, laughing. "I'll come for four dollars a month, if you'll do that."

"I never heard such impudence," said Sam, in concentrated wrath. "I never was so repaid for kindness before."

"Look here, Sam," said Ben, "I understand just how kind you are. You want the satisfaction of ordering me round, and you can't have it. I decline your offer. I'd rather beg for bread than accept it."

"You may starve, for all me," said Sam. "It's ridiculous for a poor boy to put on such airs. You'll die in the poorhouse yet."

"I won't live there, if I can help it. What! are you going to leave me?"

"I won't condescend to be seen with you."

"Good-by, Sam. I hope you won't have to black your own boots."

Sam did not deign a reply.

"He looks mad," thought Ben. "I'd live on one meal a day rather than let him order me round."

CHAPTER IV.
A BRILLIANT CHANCE.

The week was over, and Ben persisted in his determination to leave

Hampton.

"I'm sorry you are going, Ben," said his Cousin Jennie. "I shall miss you awfully."

As Jennie was the prettiest girl in the village, though she did not inherit any good looks from her plain-looking father, Ben was gratified.

"You'd forget me soon," he said.

"No, I won't."

"Especially when Sam Sturgis comes round to see you."

"I don't want to see him. He's a stuck-up boy, and thinks himself too good to associate with common people."

"He wanted to have me black his boots," said Ben.

"He isn't fit to black yours," said Jennie energetically.

"Oh, yes, he is," said Ben, laughing. "That's where you and I disagree."

"I guess we both mean about the same thing," said Jennie, who saw the point.

Ben's resolve to go to California was modified by an advertisement in a New York daily paper which he saw at the village tavern.

It ran thus:

"Wanted, six boys, from fifteen to eighteen years of age, to fill positions of trust. Ten dollars per week will be paid; but a deposit of fifty dollars is required as a guarantee of honesty. This sum will be repaid at the close of term of service. Address Fitch & Perguson, No.—Nassau Street."

This advertisement looked quite attractive to Ben. He copied it, and showed it to Uncle Job.

"Isn't that a good chance, Uncle Job?" he said. "Just think! Ten dollars a week!"

"You'd have to pay your board out of it," said his uncle.

"I know that, but my board wouldn't cost more than four dollars a week. That would leave me six."

"So it would. I declare it does seem to be a good chance. Maybe they've got all the boys they want."

"Why, you see, uncle, there's a good many boys that couldn't pay the deposit money. That would limit the number of applicants. Now, I have the money, and I guess I'd better write to New York at once about it."

"Maybe you had, Ben."

Ben immediately procured a sheet of paper and wrote to the advertisers, stating that he would like the position, and assuring them of his ability to furnish the required sum. The letter went to New York by the afternoon mail.

Naturally Ben was a little excited and suffered a little from suspense. He feared that all the places would be filled, and such another chance was hardly to be expected again very soon. However, on Monday morning he was gratified by the receipt of the following letter:

"No.—NASSAU STREET, NEW YORK.

"MR. BENJAMIN STANTON: Your letter of yesterday is at hand. Fortunately we have one vacancy, the other places being already filled. We have rejected three applicants for it on account of unsatisfactory penmanship. Yours, however, is up to the mark, and we will engage you on the strength of it. It will be necessary for you to report as soon as possible at our office for duty. We require the deposit on account of the sums of money which you will handle. We do not doubt your honesty, but it seems desirable that you should furnish a guarantee, particularly as we pay a much larger salary than is usually given to young clerks.

"Yours respectfully,

"FITCH & FERGUSON.

"P. S. Your engagement will not commence until the fifty dollars are in our hands."

Ben was quite elated by his success.

"I must start to-morrow morning," he said, "or I shall be in danger of losing the place."

"It seems very sudden," said his aunt. "I am afraid I sha'n't have time to get your clothes ready. Some are dirty, and others need mending. If I'd had a little notice-"

"It won't make any difference, Aunt Sarah," said Ben. "I'll take a few clothes in a carpetbag, and you can send the rest by express when they are ready."

"Yes, Sarah, that will be the best way," said Uncle Job. "Ben don't want to run the risk of losing the place by delay."

Mrs. Stanton acquiesced rather unwillingly, and for the remainder of the day Ben was busy making preparations to leave his country home.

CHAPTER V.

IN SEARCH OF A PLACE.

Ben took the early train to New York on Tuesday morning, and in due time arrived in the city. He carried with him seventy-five dollars out of his small patrimony. Fifty were to be deposited with Messrs. Fitch & Ferguson, as required, and the balance was to defray his expenses till he began to receive a salary. Ben didn't expect to need much of it, for at the end of a week he would be paid ten dollars for his services, and until then he meant to be very economical.

Ben had only been in New York twice before, but he happened to know his way to Nassau Street, and went there at once, with his carpetbag in his hand.

As he entered Nassau Street from Printing-House

Square, a bootblack accosted him.

"How are you, country?"

"Are you very anxious to know?" asked Ben, stopping short.

"Yes."

"I'm well enough and strong enough to give you a licking."

"Good for you, country! Have you come to stay long?"

Ben laughed. He concluded not to take offense, but to answer seriously.

"That depends on whether I get the place I am after."

"What is that?" asked the bootblack, in a friendly tone.

Now, on the way to the city, Ben had overheard a conversation between two gentlemen, relative to certain swindlers in New York, which, for the first time, had aroused in him a suspicion that possibly there might be something wrong about the firm whose advertisement he had answered. He felt the need of an adviser, and though his choice may be considered rather a strange one, he decided to consult his new acquaintance, the bootblack. He briefly told him of the advertisement, and what it offered.

The bootblack surveyed him with pitying curiosity.

"You don't mean to say you swallow all that?" he said.

"Don't you think it's all right?" asked Ben anxiously.

"Look here," said the street boy, "do you think anybody's going to pay a boy ten dollars a week, when there's hundreds ready to work for three or four? Why, a man in Pearl Street advertised last week for a boy at three dollars, and there was a whole shoal of boys went for it. I was one of 'em."

"Don't you earn more than that by your business?"

"Sometimes I do, but it ain't stiddy, and I'd rather have a place."

"Why do they advertise to give ten dollars, then?" asked our hero.

"They want to get hold of your fifty dollars," said the bootblack.

"Them fellers is beats, that's what they are."

"What had I better do?" asked Ben, in perplexity.

"Go and see 'em, and have a talk. If they're not after your fifty dollars, you'll know what it means."

"It may be all right, after all," said Ben, who did not like to give up hope.

"I may be General Grant," retorted the bootblack, "but if I know myself I ain't."

"Well, I'll go round and talk with them. Where can I meet you afterwards?"

"I'll be standin' here, if you ain't gone too long."

"What's your name?"

"Tom Cooper."

"I am Ben Stanton. Thank you for your advice."

"You're a good feller if you do come from the country. Just look out for them fellers. Don't let 'em hook you in."

"All right, Tom."

Ben moved on, watching the numbers as he walked slowly along, till he came to the one mentioned in the advertisement. There was a hallway and a staircase, with a directory of persons occupying offices on the floors above. From this Ben ascertained that Fitch & Ferguson occupied Room 17, on the fourth floor.

"I wonder what business they are in," thought our hero as he mounted the stairs. "They must have considerable or they wouldn't need so many boys-that is, if they are on the square."

Presently he stood in front of a door bearing the number 17.

He knocked for admittance.

CHAPTER VI.

MR. PITCH, THE SENIOR PARTNER.

"Come in," said a loud voice.

Ben opened the door and entered.

He found himself in a square room, almost bare of furniture. In an office chair at a table sat a dark-complexioned man of near forty. He appeared to be reading the morning paper.

"Is this the office of Fitch & Ferguson?" inquired Ben.

A glance at Ben's carpetbag indicated that he had come in answer to the advertisement, and he was received very graciously.

"Come in," said the man in the chair, smiling affably. "This is the office of Fitch & Ferguson. I am Mr. Fitch."

"My name is Stanton-Ben Stanton," said our hero. "I wrote you from

Hampton about your advertisement."

"For a boy at ten dollars a week?" suggested the dark man, with a pleasant smile.

"Yes, sir."

"We agreed to take you, did we not?" asked Mr. Fitch.

"Yes, sir."

"Have you had any business experience?" inquired Pitch.

"No, sir."

"I am sorry for that," said Mr. Fitch gravely. "Experience is important. I am not sure whether we ought to pay you ten dollars a week."

Ben did not reply. He was not so much concerned about the amount of his compensation as about the reliable character of Fitch & Ferguson.

"Still," mused Mr. Fitch, "you look like a boy who would learn fast.

What do you think about it yourself?"

"I think I could," answered Ben. "I should try to serve you faithfully."

"That is well. We want to be served faithfully," said Mr. Fitch.

"What kind of a business is it?" Ben ventured to ask, surveying the empty office with a puzzled look, which Mr. Fitch observed and interpreted aright.

"We do a commission business," he said. "Of course, we keep no stock of goods here. Business is not done in the city, my young friend, as it is in the country."

"No, I suppose not," returned our hero.

"Without entering into details as to the character of our business," said Mr. Fitch, "I may say that you would be chiefly employed in making collections. It is because considerable sums of money would pass through your hands that we require a deposit in order to protect ourselves. By the way, have you the fifty dollars with you?"

Ben admitted that he had.

Mr. Fitch's face brightened up, for he had not felt quite sure of that.

"I am glad to hear of it," he said. "It shows that you mean business. You may hand it to me, and I will give you a receipt for it."

"I would like to ask you one or two questions first," said Ben, making no movement toward his pocket.

Mr. Fitch frowned.

"Really, I fail to catch your meaning," he said, in a changed tone.

"Do you wish to enter my employ, or do you not?"

"I should like to earn ten dollars a week."

"Precisely. Then all you have to do is to hand me the fifty dollars and go to work."

"You might keep me only a week," suggested Ben.

"We shall keep you if you suit us, and you can if you try. If you are discharged, we give you back your money, and pay you for the time you work for us. That is fair, isn't it?"

"Yes, sir."

"Then we may as well settle the matter at once," and he waited for Ben to draw forth his money. Our hero would, undoubtedly, have done so, if he had not been cautioned by Tom Cooper. As it was, he could not help feeling suspicious.

"I should like to propose something to you, sir," he said.

"What is it?" asked Fitch impatiently.

"Suppose you keep five dollars a week out of my wages for ten weeks-that'll make fifty dollars-and only pay it to me when I leave you."

"Young man," said Mr. Fitch sternly, "this is trifling, and my time is too valuable for such discussion. Have you, or have you not, brought fifty dollars with you?"

"I have."

"Then you can secure the place-a place such as few New York boys are fortunate enough to fill. You must decide for yourself."

He threw himself back in his chair and looked at Ben.

"He seems very anxious about the money," thought our hero, "and I don't see any signs of any business. I'd better back out."

"There are plenty of boys who want the place," continued Fitch, trying to look indifferent.

"I guess you can give it to one of them," said Ben coolly.

Mr. Fitch could not conceal his disappointment. The fifty dollars had a great attraction for him. He saw that Ben was in earnest, for he was already opening the door to go out. He must make an effort to detain him.

"Wait a moment, my young friend. I like your appearance, and we may be disposed to take you on a little easier terms. Fifty dollars is probably a large sum to you."

Ben admitted that it was.

"Probably your means are limited?"

"Yes, sir; I am a poor boy."

"Just so. I will then relax our rules a little in your case. Of course, you won't mention it to our other boys, as it might create dissatisfaction."

"No, sir."

"We will take you on a deposit of forty dollars, then."

Ben shook his head, and moved as if to depart.

"In fact," said Mr. Fitch hastily, "I believe I will say thirty dollars, Though I am afraid my partner will blame me."

Ben was not versed in city ways, but now he distrusted Mr. Fitch more than ever.

"I would rather take a situation where no deposit is required," he said.

"But you can't get any unless you agree to accept three or four dollars a week."

"Can you afford to pay me ten dollars a week on account of my deposit?" asked Ben shrewdly.

Mr. Fitch flushed, for Ben's question was a home thrust.

"We don't want cheap boys," he said pompously. "We want boys who are worth high wages, and no others."

"And you think I am worth high wages?" asked Ben.

"I think so, but I may be mistaken."

Ben was not required to answer, for the door opened hastily, and a man entered in visible excitement.

"What is your business, sir?" asked Mr. Fitch, rather nervously.

"Are you Fitch or Ferguson?" demanded the intruder.

"I am Mr. Fitch."

"Two days ago my son, James Cameron, entered your service."

"Yes, sir."

"Where is he now?"

"We have sent him to Brooklyn to collect a bill."

"He paid you a deposit of fifty dollars?"

"Certainly. We require it as a guarantee of honesty and fidelity."

"Well, I want you to pay it back."

"I don't understand you, sir," said Mr. Fitch, looking very much disturbed. "It will be given up when your son leaves our employment."

"Well, he's going to leave it to-day," said the other.

"Can you get him another place as good? Ten dollars a week are not often paid to boys."

"No, sir; it's that that makes me suspicious. Give me back the fifty dollars, and James shall leave your employment."

"That is entirely irregular, sir," said Fitch. "Your son has been only two days in the office. At the end of the week he can leave us, and receive back his money."

"That won't do," said the angry father.

"It will have to do," said Fitch. "You are doing a very foolish thing, Mr. Cameron."

"I'll risk that."

"When your son returns from Brooklyn we will consider what can be done."

"When will that be?"

"In a couple of hours."

"I will come in then."

Cameron went out, and Ben followed him, the discomfited Fitch making no effort to detain the lad.

"I was thinking of engaging myself to Mr. Fitch," said Ben to his companion. "Do you know anything against him?"

"I hear that he's a swindler," said Cameron. "I was a fool to fall into his snare. Keep your money and you'll be better off."

"Thank you, sir."

Fifteen minutes afterward Mr. Fitch left his office, and when Mr. Cameron came back, the door was locked. He found his son waiting in the entry.

"Did you collect any money in Brooklyn?" asked his father.

"No; I guess Mr. Fitch gave me the wrong number. There was no such man living at the house he sent me to."

"We've been fooled!" said the father bitterly. "Come home, James. I doubt we've seen the last of our money. If I ever set eyes on that man Pitch again I'll give him in charge for swindling."

The senior partner of Pitch & Ferguson was at that moment on his way to Philadelphia with the remains of the fifty dollars in his pocket. But for Ben's caution he would have had another fifty dollars in his possession.

CHAPTER VII.
BEN'S DINNER-GUEST.

Ben slowly retraced his steps to where he had left his friend, Tom Cooper.

"Well," said the bootblack, "did you see Fitch and Ferguson?"

"Yes," answered Ben soberly; "that is, I saw one of them."

"Did you take the place?"

"No; I found he was too anxious for my fifty dollars, though he offered after a while to take me for thirty."

Tom Cooper laughed derisively.

"I'll do better nor that," he said. "If you'll give me twenty dollars, I'll make you my private secretary, payin' you ten dollars a week."

"How long will you keep me?" asked Ben, smiling.

"Six days," answered Tom. "Then I'll have to sack you without pay, 'cause you don't understand your business."

"Is that the way they manage?" asked Ben.

The bootblack nodded.

Ben looked grave. The disappointment was a serious one, and he felt now how much he had relied upon the promises of Fitch & Ferguson. He had formed no other plans, and it seemed likely that he must return to the country to resume his old life. Yet that seemed impracticable. There was no opening there unless he accepted one of the two offers already made him. But he was neither inclined to enter the employ of Deacon Pitkin, nor to become the valet and servant of Sam Sturgis. He was not quite sure whether he would not prefer to become a bootblack, like his new acquaintance.

"What are you goin' to do?" asked Tom.

"I wish I knew," said Ben earnestly. "What can I do?"

"You might go into my business," suggested Tom.

Ben shook his head.

"I don't think I should like that."

"No more would I if I'd got fifty dollars in my pocket. If I was you I'd go into business."

"What kind of business?"

"Well," said Tom reflectively, "you might buy out an apple or a peanut-stand, and have lots of money left."

"Is there much money to be made that way?" inquired Ben.

"Well, I never knowed anybody get rich in that line. I guess you'd make a livin'."

"That wouldn't satisfy me, Tom. What I want most of all is to go to California."

The bootblack whistled.

"That's off ever so far, isn't it?"

"Yes, it's a long way."

"How do you go?"

"There are three ways," answered Ben, who had made himself familiar with the subject. "The first is to go by land-across the plains. Then there is a line of steamers by way of Panama. The longest way is by a sailing-vessel round Cape Horn."

"What would you do when you got to California?" asked Tom.

"Go to work. I suppose I would go to the mines and dig gold."

"I wish it wasn't so far off. I'd like to go myself. Do you think a feller could work his passage?"

"By blacking boots?"

"Yes."

"I don't believe he could. Sailors don't care much about having their boots blacked."

"How much does it cost to go?"

"I don't know."

"Why don't you go to the office and find out?"

"So I will," said Ben, brightening up at the thought. "Do you know where it is?"

"Yes."

"Will you show me?"

"I would if I'd make enough to buy me some dinner. I only had a five-cent breakfast, and I feel kinder holler."

"I feel hungry myself," said Ben. "If you'll go with me I'll buy you some dinner to pay you for your trouble."

"'Nough said!" remarked Tom briefly, as he shouldered his box. "I'm your man. Come along! Where shall we go first?"

"To an eating-house. We might have to wait at the office."

Tom conducted Ben to a cheap restaurant, not far away, where the two for a moderate sum obtained a plentiful meal. Had either been fastidious, some exception might have been taken to the style in which the dishes were served, but neither was critical. A dapper young clerk, however, who sat opposite Tom, seemed quite disturbed by the presence of the bootblack. As his eye rested on Tom he sniffed contemptuously, and frowned. In truth, our friend Tom might be useful, but in his present apparel he was not fitted to grace a drawing-room. He had no coat, his vest was ragged, and his shirt soiled with spots of blacking. There were spots also upon his freckled face, of which Tom was blissfully unconscious. It didn't trouble him any to have a dirty face. "Dirt is only matter in the wrong place," as a philosopher once remarked. Tom was a philosopher in his own way.

The young clerk pulled out a scented handkerchief, and applied it to his nose, looking at Tom meanwhile.

"What's the matter of yer?" inquired Tom, suspecting the cause of the dandy's discomfort. "Be you sick?"

"It's enough to make one sick to sit at the table with you," answered the clerk.

"Why?"

"You are absolutely filthy. Don't you know any better than to come in where there are gentlemen?"

"I don't see any except him," said Tom, indicating Ben with his glance.

"This is really too much. Here, waiter!"

A waiter answered the summons.

"What is it, sir?"

"Just remove my plate to another table, will you?"

"Is anything the matter, sir?"

"I am not accustomed to associate with bootblacks," said the clerk loftily.

"All right, sir."

"I am really surprised that you admit any of that low class."

"As long as they pay their bills we are willing to receive them."

"I don't believe that boy has got enough to pay for his dinner."

The waiter, at this suggestion, looked at Tom rather suspiciously. After removing the plate of the sensitive customer, he came back to the table where the two boys were seated.

"Have you given your order?" he asked.

"Yes."

"If you haven't got money enough to pay your check you'll be bounced."

"Don't you trouble yourself, old woolly head," said Tom coolly. "My friend pays the bills. He's a banker down in Wall Street, and he's rich enough to buy out your whole place."

"The dinner will be paid for," said Ben, smiling.

"All right, gentlemen," said the waiter, more respectfully. "We'll be glad to see you any time."

"Tom," said Ben, "I'm afraid you don't always tell the truth."

"Why not?"

"You told the waiter I was a Wall Street banker, and rich."

"Oh, what's the odds? You're rich enough to pay for the dinners, and that's all he wants."

"You came near spoiling the appitite of that young man over at the opposite table."

"I'd like to spoil his beauty. He feels too big. I don't like to see a feller put on so many airs. What's the matter of me, I'd like to know?"

"Why, you see, Tom, your face isn't very clean. There are spots of blacking on it."

"A feller can't be always washin' his face. I'll wash it to-morrow mornin' at the lodge. Does it take away your appetite, too?"

"Not a bit," said Ben, laughing. "Nothing but a good dinner will take away that."

"You're the kind of feller I like," said Tom emphatically. "You don't put on no airs."

"I can't afford to," said Ben. "I'm a poor boy myself."

"I wouldn't feel poor if I had fifty dollars," returned Tom.

"I hope you'll have it sometime, and a good deal more."

"So do I. When I'm a rich man, I'll wash my face oftener."

"And put blacking on your boots instead of your face," added Ben.

"It might look better," Tom admitted.

When dinner was over the two boys directed their steps to the California steamship office, on one of the North River piers.

CHAPTER VIII.
A STRANGE ACQUAINTANCE.

Tom Cooper was too familiar with the streets of New York to pay any attention to the moving panorama of which he and Ben formed a part. But everything was new and interesting to Ben, who had passed his life in a quiet country town.

"I should think it was the Fourth of July," he said.

"Why?" asked the bootblack.

"Because there's such a lot of people and wagons in the streets."

"There's always as many as this, except Sundays," said Tom.

"Where do they all come from?" said Beu wonderingly.

"You've got me there," answered Tom. "I never thought about that. Look out!" he exclaimed suddenly, dragging Ben from in front of a team coming up the street. "Do you want to get run over?"

"I was looking the other way," said Ben, rather confused.

"You've got to look all ways to once here," said Tom.

"I guess you're right. Don't people often get run over?"

"Once in a while. There's a friend of mine—Patsy Burke—a newsboy, was run over last year and had his leg broke. They took him to Bellevue Hospital, and cut it off."

"Is he alive now?"

"Oh, yes, he's alive and to work, the same as ever. He's got a wooden leg."

"Poor boy!" said Ben compassionately.

"Oh, he don't mind it, Patsy don't. He's always jolly."

By this time they reached the office of the California Steamship Company. There was a large sign up, so that there was no difficulty in finding it.

The two boys entered. The room was not a large one. There was a counter, behind which were two young men writing, and there was besides a man of middle age, who was talking to two gentlemen who appeared to be engaging passage. Seated in a chair, apparently awaiting her turn, was a young lady, whose face was half-concealed by a thick, green veil.

When the two gentlemen were disposed of, the agent spoke to the young lady.

"What can I do for you, miss?" he asked.

"I am in no hurry, sir," she answered, in a low voice. "I will wait for those boys."

"What's your business, boys?" demanded the agent, shrugging his shoulders.

"When does the next steamer start, sir?" inquired Ben.

"In three days."

"What is the price of passage?"

"First-class?"

"No, sir, the cheapest."

"One hundred dollars. Do you wish to secure passage?"

"Not this morning, sir."

The agent shrugged his shoulders again, as if to say "I thought so," and turned again to the young lady.

"Now, miss," he said.

"I beg your pardon, sir," she said hurriedly. "I will call again."

As she spoke, she left the office, following the two boys so quickly that they almost went out together.

Ben had not taken particular notice of the young lady, and was much surprised when he felt a hand laid on his arm, and, turning, his eyes fell npon her face.

"May I speak a few words with you?" she said.

"Certainly," answered Ben politely, though he could not conceal his astonishment.

The young lady looked uneasily at Tom, and hesitated.

"Won't you move away a few steps, Tom?" said Ben, understanding the look.

"Thank you," said the young lady, in a low voice. "Are you intending to sail for California by the next steamer?"

"I should like to, miss, but I am poor, and I don't know whether I can afford the expense of a ticket."

"Would you go if your ticket were paid-by a friend?"

"You bet I would-I mean I certainly would," answered Ben, correcting his phraseology, as he remembered that he was addressing a young lady, and not one of his boy friends.

"Would you be willing to take care of me—that is, to look after me?"

Ben was certainly surprised; but he answered promptly and with native politeness: "It would be a pleasure to me."

"You were going alone-you had no friends with you?"

"None at all, miss."

"That is well," she said. "What is your name?"

"Ben Stanton."

"Do you live in the city?"

"No, miss. I came from the small town of Hampton."

"Where are you staying?"

"Nowhere. I only arrived in the city this morning."

"Will you be able to go by the next steamer?"

Ben hesitated. It almost took away his breath—it seemed so sudden-but he reflected that there really was no reason why he should not, and he answered in the affirmative.

"Then go back with me, and I will engage passage for us both."

The young lady and Ben reentered the office, Tom Cooper looking on with astonishment. She approached the counter, this time with confidence, and the agent came forward.

"I have concluded to engage passage for myself and this lad," she said.

The agent regarded her with surprise.

"Both first-class?" he asked.

"Certainly, sir. I should like the lad to occupy a stateroom near mine."

"Very well. I will show you on the plan those that are unengaged. I cannot give either of you a stateroom to yourselves. I can give you a room with a very agreeable lady, a Mrs. Dunbar, and the boy can occupy part of the adjoining room."

"Very well, sir."

"What name?" continued the agent.

"Ida Sinclair," answered the young lady, with visible hesitation.

"And the boy's name?"

Miss Sinclair had forgotten; but Ben promptly answered for himself.

The young lady drew out her pocketbook, and produced several large bills, out of which she paid the passage money. Then, turning to Ben, she said: "Now we will go."

Ben followed her out of the office, feeling completely bewildered. Well he might. The young lady had paid two hundred and fifty dollars for his passage, and for this large outlay only required him to take care of her. No wonder he thought it strange.

"You say you are not staying at any hotel?" said the young lady, as they emerged into the street.

"No, Miss Sinclair."

"I am staying at the Astor House, and it is important that you should be with me, as I may have some errands on which to employ you."

"Is it an expensive hotel?" asked Ben.

"That will not matter to you, as I shall pay the bill."

"Thank you, Miss Sinclair; but you are spending a great deal of money for me."

"I have an object in doing so. Besides, I have no lack of money."

"Shall I go with you to the hotel now?"

"Yes."

"May I speak a moment to the boy who was with me?"

"Certainly."

"May I tell him where I am going?"

"Yes, but ask him to keep it to himself."

"I will, Miss Sinclair," and Ben was about to walk away.

"On the whole, call the boy here," said Miss Sinclair. "Tom!" Tom

Cooper answered the summons.

"I am going to California with this lady," said Ben. "She has paid my passage."

"You're in luck!" exclaimed Tom. "Say, miss, you don't want a boy to go along to black your boots, do you?"

Miss Sinclair smiled faintly.

"I think not," she answered.

"Tom," continued Ben, "you won't say a word about my going, will you?"

"Not if you don't want me to. Besides, there ain't nobody to tell."

Miss Sinclair looked relieved. She drew out her pocketbook, and took from it a ten-dollar bill.

"What is your name?" she asked.

"Tom Cooper, ma'am."

"Then, Tom, allow me to offer you a small present."

"Is it all for me?" exclaimed Tom, in amazement.

"Yes."

Tom thrust it into his vest pocket, and immediately executed a somersault, rather to Miss Sinclair's alarm.

"Excuse me, ma'am," said Tom, assuming his natural posture; "I couldn't help it, I felt so excited. I never was so rich before."

"May I tell Tom where we are going to stop?" asked Ben.

"Certainly, if he will keep it to himself."

"I shall be at the Astor House, Tom. Come round and see me."

Tom watched the two as they preceded him on their way to Broadway.

"I wonder if I'm dreaming," he said to himself. "If I am, I hope I won't wake up till I've spent this ten dollars. I guess I'll go to the Old Bowery to-night."

CHAPTER IX.

AT THE ASTOR HOUSE.

As they walked up to the hotel together, Miss Sinclair said: "You are probably surprised at what has taken place, but I have strong reasons for acting as I have done."

"I don't doubt it, Miss Sinclair," returned Ben.

"It is desirable that I should tell you-"

"Don't tell me anything unless you like, Miss Sinclair. I am not troubled with curiosity."

"Thank you, but in the confidential relations which we are to hold toward each other, it is necessary that you should understand my position. I will reserve my explanation, however, till we reach the hotel."

"We are to stop at the Astor House?"

"Yes, and I wish you to put down my name and your own on the register, and obtain two rooms as near together as convenient."

"Very well, Miss Sinclair."

"You may put me down as from-well, from Philadelphia."

"All right. Shall I put myself down from Philadelphia, too?"

"Not unless you choose. Your native village will answer. By the way, you are to pass for my cousin, and it will be better, therefore, that you should call me by my first name-Ida."

"I wouldn't take the liberty but for your wishing it."

"I do wish it-otherwise it would be difficult to pass you off as my cousin."

"All right, Miss Sinclair-I mean Ida."

"That is better. I shall call you Ben."

"You couldn't very well call me Mr. Stanton," said our hero, smiling.

"Not very well. But here we are at the hotel. We will go in together. I will go to the ladies' parlor, and you can join me there after securing rooms at the office."

"Very well-Ida."

Of course Ben was not used to city hotels, and he was a little afraid that he should not go to work properly, but he experienced no difficulty. He stepped up to the desk, and said to the clerk:

"I should like to engage rooms for my cousin and myself."

The clerk pushed the register toward him.

Ben inscribed the names. At first he could not remember his companion's last name, and it made him feel awkward. Fortunately it came to him in time.

"We can give you rooms on the third floor. Will that do?"

"Yes, sir, I think so. We would like to be near together."

"Very well. I can give you two rooms directly opposite to each other."

"That will do, sir."

The clerk touched a bell, and a porter presented himself:

"Here are the keys of sixty-six and sixty-eight," said the hotel clerk. "Take this young gentleman's luggage to sixty-six, and show the lady with him to number sixty-eight."

Ben followed the porter, pausing at the door of the ladies' parlor, where his companion awaited him.

"Come, Ida," he said, feeling a little awkward at addressing Miss

Sinclair so familiarly. "The servant is ready to show us our rooms."

"Very well, Ben," said Miss Sinclair, smiling. She did not seem so nervous now.

As the clerk had said, the rooms were directly opposite each other. They were large and very comfortable in appearance. As Miss Sinclair entered her room she said:

"Join me in the ladies' parlor in fifteen minutes, Ben. I have something to say to you."

Ben looked around him with considerable satisfaction. He had only left home that morning; he had met with a severe disappointment, and yet he was now fortunate beyond his most sanguine hopes. He had heard a great deal of the Astor House, which in Hampton and throughout the country was regarded at that time as the most aristocratic hotel in New York, and now he was actually a guest in it. Moreover, he was booked for a first-class passage to California.

"It's like the Arabian Nights," thought Ben, "and Miss Sinclair must be a fairy."

He took out his scanty wardrobe from the carpetbag, and put it away in one of the drawers of the bureau.

"I might just as well enjoy all the privileges of the hotel," he said to himself.

He took out his brush and comb, and brushed his hair. Then he locked the door of No. 66 and went down-stairs to the ladies' parlor.

He did not have to wait long. In five minutes Miss Sinclair made her appearance.

"Ben," she said, "here is the check for my trunk. You may take it down to the office and ask them to send for it. Then come back and I will acquaint you with some things I wish you to know."

Ben speedily reappeared, and at Miss Sinclair's request sat down beside her on a sofa.

"You must know, Ben," she commenced, "that I am flying from my guardian."

"I hope it's all right," said Ben, rather frightened. He was not sure but he was making himself liable to arrest for aiding and abetting Miss Sinclair's flight.

"You have no cause for alarm. He has no legal control over me, though by the terms of my father's will he retains charge of my property till I attain my twenty-fifth year. Before this, fourteen months must elapse. Meanwhile he is exerting all his influence to induce me to marry his son, so that the large property of which I am possessed may accrue to the benefit of his family."

"He couldn't force you to marry his son, could he?" asked Ben.

"No, but he has made it very disagreeable to me to oppose him, and has even gone so far as to threaten me with imprisonment in a madhouse if I do not yield to his persuasions."

"He must be a rascal!" said our hero indignantly.

"He is," said Miss Sinclair quietly.

"I don't see how he can do such things in a free country."

"He has only to buy over two unscrupulous physicians, and in a large city that can easily be done. On their certificate of my insanity I might any day be dragged to a private asylum and confined there."

"I don't wonder you ran away, Ida."

"I feel perfectly justified in doing so. Liberty and the control of my own person are dear to me, and I mean to struggle for them."

"What makes you think of going to California? is it because it is so far off?"

"Partly; but there is another reason," said Miss Sinclair. "I will not conceal from you that there is a person there whom I wish to meet."

"Is it a young man?" asked Ben shrewdly.

"You have guessed it. Richard Dewey is the son of a former bookkeeper of my father. He is poor, but he is a gentleman, and there is a mutual attachment between us. Indeed, he asked my guardian's consent to his suit, but he was repelled with insult, and charged with being a fortune-hunter. That name would better apply to my guardian and his precious son."

"Is Mr. Dewey in California?"

"Yes; he went out there some months since. He promised to write me regularly, but I have not heard a word from him. I know very well that he has written, and that my guardian has suppressed his letters."

"That is shameful!" said Ben warmly.

"It is indeed; but with your help I think I can circumvent Mr.

Campbell yet."

"Mr. Campbell is your guardian, I suppose, Ida?"

"Yes."

"You may reply upon me to help you in every way possible, Miss

Sinclair."

"Ida," corrected the young lady.

"I mean Ida."

"That's right, Cousin Ben."

Now that Miss Sinclair's veil was removed, our hero could see that she was very pretty, and perhaps he felt all the more proud of being selected as her escort. But on one point he was in the dark.

"May I ask you a question, Ida?" he said. "How is it that you have chosen me-a stranger, and so young-as your escort? I am only a green country boy."

"Partly because I like your looks; you look honest and trustworthy."

"Thank you, but I am only a boy."

"That's all the better for me. It would not do for me to accept the escort of a man, and it would be awkward for me to propose it even if it would do."

"At any rate, I am lucky to be selected. I hope you will be satisfied with me."

"I feel sure of it."

"You are spending a great deal of money for me."

"You may feel surprised that I have so much money to spend independent of my guardian, but he has control only of the property left by my father. My mother left me thirty thousand dollars, of which I am sole mistress."

"That is lucky for you."

"Under present circumstances-yes."

Here two ladies entered the parlor, and the conversation was suspended.

"I believe I will go in to dinner now," said Miss Sinclair. "Will you come, Ben?"

"I ate dinner an hour ago."

"Then you can go where you please. Meet me here at six o'clock."

"All right, Ida."

CHAPTER X.
BEN RECEIVES A CALL.

Ben had scarcely left the room when it occurred to him that he ought to send home for the remainder of his clothes. He did not like to do so, however, without first consulting Miss Sinclair.

"Well, Ben?" said the young lady inquiringly.

"I would like to write home for my clothes, if you have no objection."

"Certainly; but don't say anything about me."

"All right."

Ben went to the reading-room, and, procuring writing-materials, penned the following letter to his uncle:

"ASTOR HOUSE, NEW YORK.

"DEAR UNCLE JOB: Will you send me the rest of my clothes at once, by express? You may direct to this hotel, where I am now staying. The firm that I came to see turned out to be swindlers, and I was at first quite disappointed; but I have made other friends, and am to sail for California next Saturday. This may seem sudden to you. At any rate it does to me, and I don't expect to realize it till I am fairly at sea. It will be some time before I can write you, but I will send you a line from Panama, if possible. You needn't send me any more of my money, for I have with me all I shall need at present.

"Give my love to aunt and Cousin Jenny. I should like to see you all again before I start, but I cannot spare the time. I am in good health and spirits, and I think my prospects are good. Your affectionate nephew, BEN."

This letter excited considerable surprise in Hampton.

"I'm afraid Ben's gettin' extravagant," said Uncle Job. "I've always heerd that the Astor House is a fashionable hotel where they charge big prices. Ben ought to have gone to a cheap place, and saved his money."

"He says he's got money enough with him, father," said Mrs. Stanton.

"How much did he take away with him?"

"Seventy-five dollars."

"And he had to pay his passage to California out of that?"

"Of course."

"He won't have much left when he gets to California, then."

"No, he won't."

"Don't you think you'd better send him some?"

"No, wife. Ben says no, and I'm goin' accordin' to his directions.

I suppose he knows best what he wants."

Sam Sturgis did not often condescend to notice Job Stanton, but his curiosity got the better of his pride, and, meeting the old man a short time afterward, he asked: "Have you heard anythiug from Ben?"

"Yes, he writ me a letter from New York. I got it this mornin'?"

"Has he got a chance to black boots?" asked Sam, with a sneer.

"He's stayin' at the Astor House," said Job, enjoying Sam's surprise.

"Staying at the Astor House!" exclaimed the young aristocrat in astonishment. "Why, that is a tip-top hotel."

"I always heerd it was," returned Job. "How can he afford to stay there?"

"He didn't say."

"Oh, I understand," said Sam, with an air of relief. "He's got a place to black boots, or clean knives. That must be the way of it."

"I don't think it is, for he has engaged passage to Californy."

"Is that so? When does he sail?"

"On Saturday. We're goin' to send him his clothes. Do you want to send him any word or message?"

"No; why should I?"

"I thought you was one of his friends."

"Yes, I will send him a message," said Sam. "Just tell him that when he has spent all his money, I'll give him the place I offered him before he left Hampton."

"You're very kind," said Job, concealing his amusement; "but I don't think Ben will need to take up with your offer."

"I think he will," said Sam.

"I wonder whether Ben is really staying at the Astor House, and paying his expenses there," he said to himself. "If he is, he's a fool. I've a great mind to ask father if I may go up to New York, and see. Maybe he's only humbugging his uncle."

So when Sam got home he preferred a request to visit New York, and obtained permission.

We now return to the Astor House.

Miss Sinclair and Ben went in to supper together. The young lady had scarcely taken her place, and looked around her, when she started, and turned pale.

"Ben," she said hurriedly, "I must leave the table. Do you see that tall man sitting by the window?"

"Yes, Cousin Ida."

"It is my guardian. He has not seen me yet, but I must be cautious. Direct a servant to bring me some supper in my room, and come up there yourself when you are through."

"All right!"

Miss Sinclair left the room, but Ben maintained his place. He took particular notice of the gentleman who had been pointed out to him. He was a tall, slender man, with iron-gray hair, and a stern, unpleasant look. Ben judged that her guardian had not seen Miss Sinclair, for he seemed wholly intent upon his supper.

"I don't wonder she wanted to run away from him," thought our hero. Ben smiled as it flashed upon him that this young lady was running away with him.

"I didn't expect, when I left home, to meet with any such adventure as this," he said to himself. "But I do mean to help Miss Sinclair all I possibly can. It doesn't seem quite natural to call her Ida, but I will do as she wants me to."

Meanwhile Mr. Campbell had made inquiries at the office if a young lady from Albany was staying at the hotel.

"No," said the clerk.

It will be remembered that Miss Sinclair had registered from

Philadelphia, or, rather, Ben had done so for her.

"Have you any young lady here without escort?" asked Mr. Campbell.

"No, sir. There is a young lady from Philadelphia, but she arrived with her cousin, a lad of fifteen or sixteen."

"That cannot be the one I am in search of," said the unsuspecting guardian.

Of course, as the reader will readily surmise, Ida Sinclair was not the young lady's real name, but it is the name by which we shall know her for the present.

After supper Ben went to Miss Sinclair's room, as directed.

"I think, Ben," she said, "it will be best for me to take all my meals in my room during the short time I stay here. Should my guardian catch sight of me he might give me some trouble, and that I wish to avoid."

"I guess you're right," said Ben.

"I shall wish you to come to my room two or three times a day, as I may have some errands for you to do."

"All right, Miss Sinclair."

"You had better call me 'Cousin Ida,' so as to get used to it."

The next day as Ben was standing on the steps of the hotel he saw, with surprise, Sam Sturgis approaching. It did not occur to him, however, that he was responsible for Sam's presence in the city. He was glad to see a familiar Hampton face, and he said cordially: "How are you, Sam?"

Sam nodded.

"You don't mean to say that you are stopping here, do you?"

"Yes, I do," said Ben, smiling. "Why not?"

"Because it's a first-class hotel."

"Why shouldn't I stay at a first-class hotel, Sam?"

"Because you are a poor boy. Maybe you've got some relations among the servants?"

"If I have I don't know it."

"Your uncle told me you were stopping here, but I didn't believe it."

"Do you believe it now?" asked Ben.

"Perhaps you just stay round here to make people believe you are a guest of the house."

"Why should I care what people think? Nobody knows me here. However, Sam, if you want to be convinced, just come up to my room with me."

Sam concluded to accept the invitation, and accompanied Ben to the desk.

"Please give me the key to number sixty-six," said Ben.

"Here it is, sir."

Sam began to think Ben's statement was true, after all. There was no room for doubt when Ben ushered him into the handsome chamber which he occupied.

"Make yourself at home, Sam," said Ben, enjoying his companion's surprise.

"It's very queer," thought Sam. "I wonder whether he won't run off without paying his bill."

Sam rather hoped that this might be the case, as it would involve

Ben in disgrace.

"Your uncle tells me you are going to sail for California on

Saturday."

"Yes, Sam."

"Have you bought your ticket?"

"Yes."

"How much did you pay?"

"Excuse me. I would rather not tell just now."

"I suppose he goes in the steerage," thought Sam.

As he could learn nothing more from our hero, Sam soon left him.

It was certainly remarkable that the boy to whom he had recently offered the position of his bootblack should be a guest of a fashionable New York hotel.

CHAPTER XI.

MISS SINCLAIR'S STRATAGEM.

Mr. Campbell had no particular reason to think that Miss Ida Sinclair, registering from Philadelphia, was the ward of whom he was in pursuit. Still, he thought it worth while to find out what he could about her, and managed to waylay Ben in the corridor of the hotel the next morning.

"Good morning, boy!" he said stiffly, not having the art of ingratiating himself with young people.

"Good morning, man!" Ben thought of replying, but he thought this would be hardly polite, and said: "Good morning, sir," instead.

He suspected Mr. Campbell's purpose, and resolved to answer cautiously.

"This is a nice hotel," said the guardian, resolving to come to the point by degrees.

"Yes, sir."

"I suppose you are too young to have traveled much?"

"I never traveled much, sir."

"Didn't I see you in the company of a young lady?"

"Very likely, sir."

"Your sister, I suppose?"

"No, sir."

"A relation, I suppose?"

"I call her Cousin Ida," said Ben truthfully.

"Indeed! And she is from Philadelphia?"

Ben was placed in a dilemma. He saw that he should be forced to misrepresent, and this he did not like. On the other hand, he could not tell the truth, and so betray Miss Sinclair to her persecutor.

"You can tell by looking at the hotel register," he said coldly.

Mr. Campbell judged by Ben's tone that our hero meant to rebuke his curiosity, and, having really very little idea that he was on the right track, he thought it best to apologize.

"Excuse my questions," he said, "but I have an idea that I know your cousin."

"In that case," said Ben, "if you will tell me your name I will speak to Cousin Ida about it."

Now Mr. Campbell was in a dilemma. If Ida Sinclair were really the ward of whom he was in pursuit, his name would only put her on her guard. He quickly thought of a ruse.

"I will send a card," he said.

He stepped to the clerk's desk, and asked for a blank card. After an instant's hesitation, he penciled the name James Vernon, and handed it to Ben.

"The young lady may not remember my name," he said; "but in an interview I think I can recall it to her recollection. Please give it to your cousin."

"All right, sir."

Ben went up-stairs and tapped for admission at Miss Sinclair's door.

"Well, Ben?" she said inquiringly.

"Here is a card which a gentleman down-stairs asked me to hand you."

"James Vernon!" repeated the young lady, in surprise. "Why, I don't know any gentleman of that name."

"He said you might not remember it; but he thought he could recall it to your recollection in a personal interview."

"I don't want a personal interview with any gentleman."

"Not with your guardian?" asked Ben, smiling.

"Was the man who handed you this card my guardian?"

"Yes; he tried to find out all he could from me; but wasn't very successful. Then he said he thought he knew you, and handed me this card."

"So he thinks to delude me by masquerading under a false name! He must suspect that I am his ward."

"Of course you won't see him?"

"No."

"What shall I say?"

"That I don't remember the name, and decline to see him."

"Won't that increase his suspicions?"

"I can't help it."

"Very well."

Ben went below; but thought he might as well put off the interview.

It was not till afternoon that Mr. Campbell met him again.

"Did you deliver my card, boy?" he asked.

"My name is Benjamin," returned our hero, who did not fancy the manner of address.

"Very well. Did you deliver my card, Benjamin?"

"Yes, sir."

"What did your cousin say?"

"That she knew no gentleman or family of your name."

"I did not expect she would remember; but I have reasons for asking an interview."

"You mustn't be offended, sir; but she declines to meet a stranger."

Mr. Campbell was baffled.

"She mistakes my motive," he said, in a tone expressive of annoyance. "How long do you stay here?"

"I can't say, sir," said Ben coldly.

Mr. Campbell bit his lip and walked away. He did not fancy being foiled by a boy. It occurred to him, however, that by waiting patiently he might see the young lady at dinner. He kept watch, therefore, till he saw Ben entering the dining-room, and then, entering himself, secured a seat near-by. But the young lady, greatly to his chagrin, did not appear. Ben observed his vigilant watch, and after dinner reported to Miss Sinclair.

The young lady smiled.

"I have thought of a way to deceive him and quiet his suspicions," she said.

Ben looked curious.

"If I remain away from the table he will feel sure that I am his ward."

"Yes, I suppose so."

"Listen to my plan, then. I have the New York Herald here, with half a column of advertisements of seamtresses. I will give you a list of three, and you shall engage one to be here early to-morrow morning. Select one with a figure as much like mine as possible."

"All right!"

"I see you look puzzled," said Miss Sinclair, smiling.

"I am, a little; I don't know what good that will do."

"Then I will explain. I shall dress the seamstress in one of my own dresses, and let her go to the table with you. Mr. Campbell will naturally suppose that she is Miss Ida Sinclair, and will be satisfied."

"I see! That is splendid!" exclaimed Ben, entering with hearty enthusiasm into the conspiracy.

It happened, luckily, that the first seamstress on whom he called was sufficiently like Miss Sinclair in figure to justify him in engaging her. He directed her to call at the hotel at eight the next morning without fail. The poor girl was glad to make this engagement, having been without employment for two weeks previous.

When she arrived, Miss Sinclair, without confiding too much in her, made known her desire, and the girl, who had had but a scanty breakfast, was glad to embrace the opportunity of enjoying the hospitality of a first-class hotel. Miss Sinclair had really work enough to employ her during the day.

When Mr. Campbell caught sight of Ben approaching the dining-room in company with a young lady, he advanced eagerly and peered into the young lady's face. He turned away in disappointment.

"I have made a fool of myself. It is only a common country girl. I must look elsewhere for my ward."

Directly after breakfast Ben had the satisfaction of seeing the obnoxious guardian depart in a hack.

"Good-by, Mr. Vernon!" he said politely. "I see you are leaving the hotel."

"Good-by!" muttered Campbell.

"I hope you'll excuse my cousin for not seeing you?"

"I don't think she's the one I supposed," said Campbell. "It's of no consequence."

Ben hastened to inform Miss Sinclair of her guardian's departure.

"Now the field is clear," said Ida, breathing a sigh of relief.

"I say, Ida, you managed him tip-top," said Ben admiringly. "I never should have thought of such a plan."

Miss Sinclair smiled faintly.

"I don't like to employ deceit," she said, "but it seems necessary to fight such an enemy with his own weapons."

"He wanted to deceive you. He put a wrong name on his card."

"That is true, Ben. I must thank you for the manner in which you have aided me in this matter. I should not have known how to act if I had not had you to call upon."

Ben's face brightened.

"I am glad to hear you say that, Cousin Ida," he said. "You are spending so much money for me that I shall be glad to feel that I have earned some of it."

"Have no trouble on that score, Ben. I foresee that you will continue to be of great service to me. I regard the money expended for you as well invested."

Ben heard this with satisfaction. It naturally gave him a feeling of heightened importance when he reflected that a wealthy heiress had selected him as her escort and right-hand man, and that she was satisfied with her choice.

On Saturday morning Miss Sinclair and Ben went on board the California steamer, and when the tide served, they started on their long voyage.

CHAPTER XII.

IN SAN FRANCISCO.

Ben was not seasick, and enjoyed the novel experiences vastly. Miss Sinclair was less fortunate. For four days she was sick and confined to her stateroom. After that she was able to appear among the other passengers. Ben was very attentive, and confirmed the favorable opinion she had already formed of him.

At last the voyage came to a close. It was a bright, cheery morning when the steamer came within sight of San Francisco. It was not a populous and brilliant city as at present, for Ben's expedition dates back to the year 1856, only a few years after the discovery of gold. Still, there was a good-sized town on the site of the future city. The numerous passengers regarded it with rejoicing hearts, and exchanged hopeful congratulations. Probably with the exception of Miss Sinclair, all had gone out to make or increase their fortunes. Her fortune was already made. She had gone to enjoy personal liberty, and to find her plighted husband.

"Well, Ben, we have nearly reached our destination," said Miss Sinclair, as she looked earnestly in the direction of the embryo city. "You are glad, are you not?"

"Yes, Cousin Ida," said Ben slowly.

"But you look thoughtful. Is there anything on your mind?"

"I feel sorry that I am to part from you, Cousin Ida."

"Thank you, Ben, but we are not to part permanently. You don't mean to forsake me utterly?"

"Not if you need me," said our hero.

"I shall still require your services. You remember that I came out here in search of a—friend?" said Miss Sinclair, hesitating.

"Yes, I know, Cousin Ida."

"I am desirous that he should know that I am in San Francisco, but, unfortunately, though I know he is in California, I have no idea where, or in what part of it he is to be found. Once in communication with him, I need have no further apprehension of interference or persecution on the part of my guardian."

"To be sure," said Ben straightforwardly. "I suppose you would marry him?"

"That may come some time," said Miss Sinclair, smiling, "but he must be found first."

"You will travel about, I suppose?" said Ben.

"No; I shall engage some one to travel for me. It would not be suitable for a young lady to go from one mining-camp to another."

"Have you thought of any one you can send?" asked our hero.

"Yes," said Miss Sinclair. "He is rather young, but I shall try the experiment."

"Do you mean me?" asked Ben quickly.

"Yes; are you willing to be my agent in the matter?"

"I should like it of all things," said Ben, with sparkling eyes.

"Then you may consider yourself engaged. The details we will discuss presently."

"And where will you stay, Cousin Ida?"

"In San Francisco. I have become acquainted with a lady on board who proposes to open a boarding-house in the city, or, rather, to take charge of one already kept by her sister. In my circumstances, it will be better for me to board with her than at a hotel. There I shall have a secure and comfortable home, while you are exploring the mining-districts in my interest."

"That is an excellent plan," said Ben.

"So I think."

Here the conversation was interrupted by the bustle of approaching departure. Ben landed in the company of Miss Sinclair and Mrs. Armstrong, and the three proceeded at once to the boarding-house, over which the latter was in future to preside. A comfortable room was assigned to Miss Sinclair, and a small one to Ben. They were plainly furnished, but both enjoyed being on land once more.

Our young hero, finding that his services were not required for the present, began to explore the city. It was composed almost wholly of wooden houses; some but one story in height, even on the leading streets, with here and there sand-hills, where now stand stately piles and magnificent hotels. He ascended Telegraph Hill, which then, as now, commanded a good view of the town and harbor; yet how different a view from that presented now. Ben was partly pleased and partly disappointed. Just from New York, he could not help comparing this straggling village on the shores of the Pacific with the even then great city on the Atlantic coast. He had heard so much of San Francisco that he expected something more. To-day a man may journey across the continent and find the same comfort, luxury, and magnificence in San Francisco which he left behind him in New York.

In his explorations Ben came to a showy building which seemed a center of attraction. It seemed well filled, and people were constantly coming in and going out. Ben's curiosity was excited.

"What is that?" he asked of a man who lounged outside, with a Mexican sombrero on his head and his hands thrust deep in his pockets.

"That's the Bella Union, my chicken."

"I don't know any better now."

"Just go in there with a pocketful of gold-dust, like I did, and you'll find out, I reckon."

"Is it a gambling-house?" inquired Ben, rather excited, for he had heard much of such places, but never seen one.

"It's the devil's den," said the man bitterly. "I wish I'd never seen it."

"Have you been unlucky?"

"Look here, boy, jest look at me," said the stranger. "An hour ago I was worth a thousand dollars in gold-dust-took six months' hard work to scrape it together at the mines-now I haven't an ounce left."

"Did you lose it there?" asked Ben, somewhat startled.

"Well, I staked it, and it's gone."

"Have you nothing left?"

"Not an ounce. I haven't enough to pay for a bed."

"What will you do for a place to sleep?" inquired Ben, to whom this seemed an alarming state of things.

The stranger shrugged his shoulders.

"I don't worry about that," he said. "I'll stretch myself out somewhere when night comes. I'm used to roughing it."

"Won't you get cold sleeping out of doors?" asked Ben.

The other gave a short, quick laugh.

"What do you take me for, boy? I don't look delicate, do I?"

"Not very," answered Ben, smiling.

"I've slept out under the stars pretty reg'lar for the past six months. I only wish I was back to the mines."

"Do you think I can go in?" Ben said hesitatingly.

"Yes, youngster, there's nothin' to bender, but take a fool's advice, and ef you've got money in your pocket, don't do it."

"You don't think I'd gamble, do you?" said Ben, horror-struck.

"I've seen youngsters smaller than you bet their pile."

"You won't catch me doing it. I am a poor boy, and have nothing to lose."

"All right, then. You're a country boy, ain't you?"

"Yes."

"So was I once, but I've had the greenness rubbed off'n me. I was jest such a youngster as you once. I wish I could go back twenty years."

"You're not very old yet," said Ben, in a tone of sympathy. "Why don't you reform?"

"No, I'm not old-only thirty-six-and I ain't so bad as I might be. I'm a rough customer, I expect, but I wouldn't do anything downright mean. Ef you're goin' into this den, I'll go with you. I can't take care of myself, but mayhap I can keep you out of danger."

"Thank you, sir."

So Ben and his new acquaintance entered the famous gambling-den. It was handsomely furnished and decorated, with a long and gaily appointed bar, while the mirrors, pictures, glass, and silverware excited surprise, and would rather have been expected in an older city. There were crowds at the counter, and crowds around the tables, and the air was heavy with the odor of Chinese punk, which was used for cigar-lights, The tinkle of silver coin was heard at the tables, though ounces of gold-dust were quite as commonly used in the games of chance.

"I suppose a good deal of money is won here?" said Ben, looking around curiously.

"There's a good deal lost," said Ben's new acquaintance.

"Gentlemen, will you drink with me?" said a young man, with flushed face, rising from a table near-by, both hands full of silver and gold, "I've been lucky to-night, and it's my treat."

"I don't care if I do," said Ben's companion, with alacrity, and he named his drink.

"What'll the boy have?"

"Nothing, thank you," answered Ben, startled,

"That won't do. I insist upon your drinking," hiccuped the young man, who had evidently drunk freely already. "Take it as a personal insult, if you don't."

"Never mind the boy," said his new friend, to Ben's great relief.

"He's young and innocent. He hasn't been round like you an' me."

"That's so," assented the young man, taking the remark as a compliment. "Well, here's to you!"

"I wouldn't have done it," said Ben's new friend rejoining him; "but it'll help me to forget what a blamed fool I've been to-night. You jest let the drink alone. That's my advice."

"I mean to," said Ben firmly. "Do people drink much out here?"

"Whisky's their nat'ral element," said the miner. "Some of 'em don't drink water once a month. An old friend of mine, Joe Granger, act'lly forgot how it tasted. I gave him a glass once by way of a joke, and he said it was the weakest gin he ever tasted."

"Are there no temperance societies out here?" asked Ben.

The miner laughed.

"It's my belief that a temperance lecturer would be mobbed, or hung to the nearest lamppost," he answered.

It is hardly necessary to say that even in 1856 intemperance was hardly as common in California as the statements of his new friend led Ben to suppose. His informant was sincere, and spoke according to his own observation. It is not remarkable that at the mines, in the absence of the comforts of civilization, those who drink rarely or not at all at home should seek the warmth and excitement of drink.

"What's your name, boy?" asked the miner abruptly.

"Ben Stanton."

"Where were you raised?"

Though the term was a new one to Ben, he could not fail to understand it.

"In the State of Connecticut."

"That's where they make wooden nutmegs," said the miner, "isn't it?"

"I never saw any made there," answered Ben, smiling.

"I reckon you've come out here to make your fortin?"

"I should like to," answered Ben; "but I shall be satisfied if I make a living, and a little more."

"You'll do it. You look the right sort, you do. No bad habits, and willin' to work hard, and go twenty-four hours hungry when you can't help it."

"Yes."

"Where'll you go first?—to the mines, I reckon."

"Yes," answered Ben, reflecting that he would be most likely to find Richard Dewey at some mining-settlement.

"Ef I hadn't been a fool, and lost all my money, I'd go along with you."

"I should like the company of some one who had already been at the mines," said Ben.

Then it occurred to him that his new acquaintance might possibly have encountered Dewey in his wanderings. At any rate, it would do no harm to inquire.

"Did you ever meet a man named Dewey at the mines?" he asked.

"Friend of yours?"

"No; I never saw him, but I have promised to hunt him up. I have some important news for him."

"Dewey!" mused the miner. "Somehow that name sounds familiar like. Can you tell what he was like?"

"I never saw him, but I can get a description of him."

"I'm sure I've met a man by that name," said the miner thoughtfully, "but I can't rightly locate him. I have it," he added suddenly. "It was at Murphy's, over in Calaveras, that I came across him. A quiet, stiddy young man-looked as if he'd come from a city-not rough like the rest of us-might have been twenty-seven or twenty-eight years old-didn't drink any more'n you do, but kept to work and minded his own business."

"That must be the man I am after," said Ben eagerly. "Do you think he is at Murphy's now?"

"How can I tell? It's most a year sence I met him. Likely he's gone. Miners don't stay as long as that in one place."

Ben's countenance fell. He did not seem as near to the object of his journey as he at first thought. Still, it was something to obtain a clue. Perhaps at Murphy's he might get a trace of Dewey, and, following it up, find him at last.

"How far is Murphy's from here?" he asked.

"Two hundred miles, I reckon."

"Then I'd better go there first."

"Not ef you want to find gold. There's other places that's better, and not so far away."

"It may be so, but I care more to find Richard Dewey than to find gold in plenty."

"You said he wasn't a friend of yours?" said the miner, in some surprise.

"No; I don't know him, but I am engaged by a friend of his to find him. That friend will pay; my expenses while I am on the road."

"Has Dewey come into a fortin?" asked the miner. "Has a rich uncle died and left him all his pile?"

"Not that I know of," answered Ben.

"Then there's a woman in it?" said his new acquaintance, in a tone of conviction. "It's his sweetheart that wants to find him. I'm right. Yes, I know it. But there's one thing that I can't see through."

"What is that?"

"Why does the gal-if it is a gal-send a boy like you on the trail?"

"Suppose there was no one else to send," suggested Ben.

"That makes it a little plainer. Where is the gal?"

"Ought I to confide in this man?" thought Ben. "I never met him before. I only know that he has lost all his money at the gambling-table. Yet he may help me, and I must confide in somebody. He is a rough customer, but he seems honest and sincere."

"Here in San Francisco," he answered. "I cannot tell you more until

I have her permission."

"That's all right. Ef I can help you, I will, Ben. You said your name was Ben?"

"Yes."

"Mine is Bradley-Jake Bradley. I was raised in Kentucky, and I've got an old mother living there now, I hope. I haven't heard anything from her for nigh a year. It makes me homesick when I think of it. Got a mother, Ben?"

"Neither father nor mother," answered Ben sadly.

"That's bad," said the miner, with rough sympathy. "You're a young chap to be left alone in the world."

"Yes; I do feel very lonely sometimes, Mr. Bradley."

"Don't call me Mr. Bradley. I ain't used to it. Call me Jake."

"All right, I'll remember it. Where can I meet you again, Jake?"

"Here will do as well as anywhere."

"Will you be here to-morrow morning at nine o'clock?"

"Yes," answered Bradley. "I'll ask the porter to call me early," he added, with rough humor.

Ben remembered that his new acquaintance had no money to pay for a night's lodging, and would be forced to sleep out.

"Can't I lend you enough money to pay for a lodging?" he asked.

"You kin, but you needn't. Jake Bradley ain't that delicate that it'll hurt him to sleep out. No, Ben, save your money, and ef I actilly need it I'll make bold to ask you for it; but I don't throw away no money on a bed."

"If you hadn't lost your money in there," said Ben, pointing to the building they had just left, "wouldn't you have paid for a bed?"

"I might have put on a little style then, I allow. It don't do for a man with a thousand dollars in his belt to lie out. I ain't afraid now."

Ben, on leaving his new acquaintance, thought it best to go back at once to Miss Sinclair, to communicate the information he had obtained, rightly deeming it of importance.

"Well, Ben, have you seen the whole town so soon?" asked Miss

Sinclair, looking up from her trunk, which she was unpacking.

"No, Cousin Ida, but I think I have learned something of Mr. Dewey."

"You have not seen him?" asked Miss Sinclair quickly.

"No, I have not seen him, but I have seen a man who met him nearly a year since at the mines."

"Tell me about it, Ben," said the young lady. "Where was it that this man saw Richard-Mr. Dewey?"

"At Murphy's."

"Where is that?"

"Two hundred miles away."

"That is not far. Are you willing to go there?"

"Yes, but you must remember, Cousin Ida, that it is nearly a year since he was there, and miners never stay long in one place, at least so my miner friend tells me."

"At any rate, you may learn something of him there."

"That is true."

"Will this man go with you?"

"He would, but he has no money to get out of the city."

"I will pay his expenses as far as Murphy's, and farther, if he is likely to prove of service."

"I think it will be best, if you can afford it," said Ben. "He knows the country, and I don't. Three months from now I should be willing to start off alone, but now-"

"It is much better that you should have company."

"It will cost you a good deal of money, Cousin Ida."

"I shall not grudge a large sum, if need be, to find Richard. When can you see this man again?"

"To-morrow morning."

"Bring him here, and I will make arrangements with him."

CHAPTER XIII.
PRELIMINARY ARRANGEMENTS.

At nine o'clock on the following morning Ben found Jake Bradley at the appointed rendezvous.

"You're on time, my lad," said Jake. "I didn't know as you'd think it worth while to look me up."

"I promised," said Ben.

"And you've kept your promise. That's more'n many a man would do."

"How did you pass the night?" asked Ben.

"I stretched out on the soft side of a board. It isn't the first time. I slept like a top."

"Have you had breakfast?"

"Well, there! you've got me," said Jake. "I reckoned on findin' an old friend that keeps a saloon on Montgomery Street, but he's sold out to another man, and I hadn't the face to ask him for a bite. What a consarned fool I was to throw away all my pile."

"Where is the saloon?" said Ben. "We will go there, and while you are eating we can arrange our business."

"Thank you, boy. I ain't above acceptin' a favor of you, and I allow that I'm empty, and need fillin' up."

"You needn't thank me, Mr. Bradley-"

"Jake!"

"Jake, then. I am only acting as the agent of Miss Sinclair."

"The gal you spoke of?"

Ben nodded.

"Then you can thank her. If there's anything I kin do for her, jest let me know."

"I mean to. That is the business I want to speak to you about."

After a hearty breakfast the two turned their steps to the private boarding-house where Miss Sinclair was eagerly awaiting them. Though Jake referred to her as "the gal," in his conversation with Ben, he was entirely respectful when brought face to face with the young lady.

"I want to thank you for my breakfast, miss, first of all," said the miner. "If I hadn't been such a thunderin' fool, I needn't have been beholden to any one, but-"

"You are entirely welcome, Mr. Bradley," said the young lady. "Ben tells me that you know something of Richard Dewey."

"Yes, miss."

"He is a valued friend of mine, and I am anxious to hear all that you can tell me of him. You don't know where he is now?"

"No, miss."

"When did you see him?"

"Nigh on to a year ago."

"That is a long time. You have heard nothing of him since?"

"No, miss. I should say yes," he added, with sudden recollection. "One of our boys saw him some months later, and reported that he was well and prosperin'. I disremember where he was, but somewhere at the mines."

"That is something. Do you think you could find him?"

"I could try, miss,"

"I am going to send out Ben, but he is only a boy. I should like to have you go with him. You know the country, and he does not. Besides, you have seen Mr. Dewey."

"Yes, I should know him ag'in if I met him."

"How did he seem when you knew him?" asked Ida, hesitating, because conscious that the question was vaguely expressed and might not be understood.

"He was a quiet, sober chap, workin' early and late," answered Jake, who, rough as he was, comprehended the drift of her questions. "He wasn't exactly pop'lar with the boys, because he wouldn't drink with 'em, and that made them think he was proud, or grudged the expense."

"They were very greatly mistaken," said Ida hastily.

"We found that out," said the miner. "A young chap fell sick; he was a newcomer and had neither friends nor money, and was pretty bad off. Dewey sat up with him night after night, and gave him fifty dollars when he got well to help him back to 'Frisco. You see, his sickness made him tired of the mines."

"That was like Richard," said Ida softly. "He was always kind-hearted."

"After that," continued Jake, "none of us had a word to say agin' him. We knowed him better, and we liked him for his kindness to that young chap."

If Jake Bradley had sought to commend himself to Ida Sinclair, he could not have found a better or more effectual way than by praising her lover. She became more cordial at once, and better satisfied with the arrangement she had formed to send off the ex-miner in Ben's company in search of her lover.

The arrangements were speedily made. The two were to start out, equipped at Miss Sinclair's expense, on an exploring-tour, the main object being to find Richard Dewey, and apprise him of her arrival in California. They were permitted, however, to work at mining, wherever there was a favorable opportunity, but never to lose sight of the great object of their expedition. From time to time, as they had opportunity, they were to communicate with Miss Sinclair, imparting any information they might have gathered.

"I shall have to leave much to your discretion," said Ida, addressing them both. "I know absolutely nothing of the country, and you, Mr. Bradley, are tolerably familiar with it. I have only to add that should you become unfortunate, and require more money, you have only to let me know. In any event, I shall take care to recompense you for all your efforts in my behalf."

"We don't want to bear too heavy on your purse, miss," said Jake

Bradley. "Once we get to the mines, we kin take care of ourselves.

Can't we, Ben?"

"I hope so, Mr. Bradley."

Bradley eyed Ben reproachfully, and our hero at once smilingly corrected himself. "I mean Jake."

"That suits me better. I s'pose the young lady wouldn't like to call me Jake?"

"I think not," said Ida, smiling.

"I ain't used to bein' called mister. The boys always called me

Jake."

"But I am not one of the boys, Mr. Bradley," said Miss Sinclair.

"Right you are, miss, and I reckon Richard Dewey would rather have you as you are."

Ida laughed merrily. To her the miner was a new character, unlike any she had ever met, and though rough and unconventional, she was disposed to like him.

"Find him for me, and you can ask him the question if you like. Tell him from me-but you must first know me by my real name."

Ben looked surprised. He had forgotten that Ida Sinclair was only assumed to elude the vigilance of her guardian.

"My real name is Florence Douglas. I am of Scotch descent, as you will judge. Can you remember the name?"

"I can, Cousin Ida-I mean Cousin Florence," said Ben.

"Then let Ida Sinclair be forgotten. Richard—Mr. Dewey-would not know me by that name."

"I tell you, Ben, that gal's a trump!" said Jake Bradley enthusiastically, when they were by themselves; "and so I'll tell Dick Dewey when I see him."

"She's been a kind friend to me, Jake. I hope we can find Mr. Dewey for her."

"We'll find him if he's in California," answered Jake.

CHAPTER XIV

THE CANON HOTEL.

Late in the afternoon of the third day subsequent a man and a boy might have been seen riding slowly through a rocky canon probably eighty miles west from San Francisco. Both were mounted on the small native horses of California, generally called mustangs. These animals possess a strength disproportioned to their size, and show great endurance. At times they have a playful habit of bucking, not quite agreeable to an inexperienced horseman.

The reader will already have guessed that the two riders are Jake Bradley and Ben. The mustangs were on a walk, being apparently weary with the day's tramp.

"Well, Ben," said Bradley, "what do you say to camping out for the night?"

"I have no objection," said Ben, "and I don't think my horse has."

"He is better off than mine, having less to carry. Are you tired?"

"Not very tired, but my limbs are rather stiff."

"What hotel shall we put up at, Ben?" asked Bradley, with a humorous glance about him.

"There isn't much choice," said Ben. "The Canon Hotel seems to be the only one that is open hereabouts. The only objection is, that we shall have to sleep on the floor, with the windows all open."

"That's about so, Ben," assented Bradley, laughing. "I shouldn't mind sleeping in a Christian bed to-night myself. Well, here goes!"

As he spoke, he jumped from the back of his horse, and, taking out a rope, tethered it to a tree hard by.

Ben followed his example.

"Now for the grub," said Bradley. "I'm powerfully empty myself. This ridin' all day up and down hill is wearin' to the stomach. What do you say?"

"I've got a healthy appetite myself, Jake."

"This yere Canon Hotel that you was talkin' about ain't first-class. It don't supply anything but cold victuals. Now, ef we had a cup of coffee to wash it down, and kinder warm us up, it would go to the right spot, eh, Ben?"

"You are right, Jake! but please don't speak of it again. It makes my mouth water."

"Stay here a few minutes, Ben, and I'll reconnoiter a little.

Perhaps I can find a better place for campin'."

"All right, Jake!"

While Bradley was absent Ben threw himself on the ground, and began to think. It was the third day of the expedition. Ben enjoyed riding through this new, unsettled country. He almost felt in the solitudes of the woods and hills as if he were the original explorer of this far-distant country. He was more than three thousand miles away from his native town, entrusted with a mission of importance. The thought was gratifying to his boyish fancy, and inspired him with a new sense of power and increased his self-reliance. He was glad, however, to have the company of Jake Bradley. He was ready to acknowledge that his chances of success, had he started alone, would have been much smaller, and certainly he would have found it exceedingly lonesome.

His companion was not a man of culture, nor were his tastes elevated, but there was a rough honesty about him, and a good humor, which made him an agreeable companion. Besides, he knew the country, and Ben felt secure in leaving the conduct of the trip to him.

"I am glad I came out here," thought Ben, as, with his head pillowed on his knapsack, he looked up through the branches of the tall trees to the blue sky beyond. "It's better than staying at home and working for Deacon Pitkin, or blacking boots for Sam Sturgis. Here I am my own man, free and don't need to run at anybody's bidding."

Probably most boys of Ben's age share his love of independence, but it is neither practicable nor desirable that at sixteen a boy should be his own master, much as he may desire it. In the case of our hero, circumstances had thrown him upon his own resources, and it may be added that he could better be trusted with the management of himself than most boys.

Ben's reverie was broken in upon by the return of his companion.

"What are you dreamin' about, Ben?" queried Jake.

"I was thinking about home, Jake."

"This don't look much like it, eh, Ben?"

"Not much."

"Well, my lad, I've found something," continued Bradley.

"Found something? What! a nugget?" exclaimed Ben, in excitement.

"Not much. This ain't the place for such a find as that."

"What, then, Jake?"

"I've found a hotel."

"Where?" asked Ben eagerly.

"Get up and stand by me. There! look yonder. What do you see?"

"It looks like smoke."

"It is smoke. There's a cabin yonder. I've reconnoitered, and I seed the door open, and a woman inside. Now, I'm going to ask her to give us some supper and a bed. Won't that be fine?"

"Splendid, Jake!"

"Then unhitch that animal of yours, and we'll put our best foot forrards, and maybe we'll get a hot supper and a Christian bed to sleep in."

CHAPTER XV.

A POLITE HOSTESS.

The cabin was a rough one, built of logs, with an adobe chimney. It contained two rooms and a loft. The inducements to live in such a lonely spot must have been small enough, but so many undesirable localities are inhabited, that it is hardly worth while to feel or express surprise at men's taste in such matters.

The approach of Ben and his companion was not observed by the inmate or inmates of the cabin. It was only when Bradley, dismounting from his mustang, struck the door-post with the handle of his whip-for it is needless to say that bells were not to be found in that neighborhood—that their presence became known.

A woman, tall, spare, and with harsh features, came to the door. She eyed Bradley askance.

"Well, what's wanted, and who are you?" she demanded.

"We are bound for the mines, ma'am," said Bradley. "We expected to camp out to-night, but we happened to see the smoke rising from your chimbly, and we made bold to ride up and ask you for supper and a night's lodging."

"We don't take in tramps," said the woman roughly.

"We're on a tramp," said Bradley, resolved not to be rebuffed, "but we've got money to pay for our accommodations."

"This ain't a hotel," said the woman, but less roughly.

"Of course not," said Bradley, in a conciliatory manner; "but I guess you won't object to get us some supper and give us a bed. We'll pay for all the trouble we make. That's fair, ain't it?"

"I don't know what my husband will say," returned the woman, in an undecided manner.

"Won't you ask him, ma'am?"

"He's gone out just now. He won't be back for an hour."

"While you're waitin' for him, can't you get us some supper? Then you can send us off if he ain't willin' to keep us."

"I'll do that," said the woman. "You'd better stay outside till I get supper ready. There ain't much room here, and you'll be in the way."

"Jest as you say, ma'am. I s'pose it would be too much to ask if you kin give us a hot cup of coffee. We haven't tasted any since we left 'Frisco."

"I can give you coffee," answered the woman. "My husband likes it, and we always keep it on hand."

"Good!" said Bradley, his face lighting up with satisfaction. "We've rid far to-day, and a cup of coffee will go to the right spot."

Bradley and Ben threw themselves on the ground near-by, and awaited with complacence the call to supper.

"We're in luck, Ben," said his companion. "Who'd have expected a hot supper out here in this lonely place?"

"I don't much like the looks of our landlady, Jake," said Ben.

"She ain't handsome, I allow, Ben; but if she gives us a good supper, that don't matter. We must make the most of this, for it's uncertain when we get another."

"W'on't she give us breakfast in the morning?"

"I didn't think of that. Maybe she will, and that'll be a good start on our to-morrow's journey."

In about three-quarters of an hour the woman came to the door, and called the travelers in to supper.

An unpainted wooden table was set in the middle of the floor, on which was spread a simple but appetizing meal. There was a plate of meat, which appeared to have been fried; a loaf of bread, and a pot of coffee; but there was neither milk nor butter. This naturally detracted from the attractiveness of the bread and coffee, but our travelers were not disposed to be fastidious.

Ben tasted the meat, and it evidently puzzled him. In taste it differed from anything he had eaten before.

Bradley smiled at his perplexity.

"Don't you know what it is, Ben?" he asked.

"No."

"Do you like it?"

"I am hungry enough to enjoy anything."

"Well, lad, it's bear steak."

"Bear steak!" repeated Ben, in surprise.

"Exactly. I've eaten it before two or three times. You see, we haven't any markets here to depend on, and we must take what we can get."

"It isn't bad," said Ben meditatively.

During this conversation the landlady had been out of the room. As it concluded, she reentered.

"Your supper is good, ma'am," said Bradley.

"Now if you only had a cow to supply you with milk and butter, you'd be fixed complete."

"If you want 'em you'll have to go somewhere else," said the woman.

"Excuse me, ma'am. I wasn't complainin' of the fare-not by no means.

I was only thinkin' of you."

"There's no call to think of me, stranger."

"Have you lived long in these parts, ma'am?" inquired Bradley socially.

"Fools ask questions, and fools answer them. I ain't a fool," responded the polite hostess.

"Excuse my curiosity, ma'am. I didn't know that it would be disagreeable to you to answer."

"Who told you it was?"

"I thought from your way of speakin'."

"It's none of your business, that's all," said the hostess.

Even Bradley was silenced. It was clear that their hostess was not inclined to be social. The remainder of the meal passed in silence.

CHAPTER XVI.
A NEW ACQUAINTANCE.

After supper the two travelers emerged from, the cabin and stretched themselves out under the trees once more. Bradley produced a clay pipe, filled the bowl with tobacco, and began to smoke.

"It's a pity you don't smoke, Ben," he said, his face expressing the satisfaction he felt.

"Would you advise me to, Jake?" questioned our hero.

"No, Ben; I guess you're better off without it; but there's nothing makes me feel so good as a smoke after a good supper."

"I feel comfortable without it, Jake."

"Then let well enough alone. I wonder whether our sweet-tempered hostess is goin' to give us a bed to-night. Not that it matters much. I'd rather have a good supper, and sleep under the trees, than have the best bed in Californy without the supper."

Here their attention was drawn to a man who was leisurely approaching. He was dressed roughly in a red shirt, trousers tucked in his boots, and a hat with a broad flapping brim. As he strode along, his revolver and bowie-knife were carelessly exposed. His complexion was dark; he wore an abundant beard, and whatever he might be, he looked like a desperado, whom one would not care to meet on a dark night, unless well armed and on the alert.

He stopped short when he caught sight of the two travelers.

"Who are you?" he asked abruptly.

"We're bound for the mines," answered Bradley. "Your good lady, if so be as you live there—indicating the cabin-has just provided us with a capital supper."

The newcomer glanced toward the door of the cabin, at which the woman now made her appearance.

"Givin' you some supper, eh? I hope she's saved some for me."

"Yes, Jack," said his wife, in a conciliatory tone; "there's plenty for you. These strangers offered to pay well for supper and lodging, and I thought you wouldn't object. I gave them the supper, but I wouldn't say anything about the lodging until you came."

"Well, stir round, old gal, and get me something to eat, for I'm dead hungry."

"Supper is ready now, Jack."

The man entered his cabin, and the next twenty minutes were consumed in repairing the ravages of hunger.

"How do you like his looks, Jake?" asked Ben, in a low voice.

"He's just the sort of man I'd expect to find in a State prison," answered Bradley. "That man's a rascal, if looks mean anything."

"I'll tell you what he reminds me of, Jake. Did you ever read

'Oliver Twist'?"

"All of a Twist? That's a queer name. What is it?"

"It's a story by Dickens. He describes a brutal villain, named Bill

Sykes, who murders his wife."

"This chap looks as if he wouldn't mind doing it. His wife's afraid of him, though half an hour ago I would have said she wasn't afraid of anything."

"That's so. They seem pretty well matched."

Presently the master of the cabin came out. It was not easy for his harsh features to look amiable, but his manner was no longer offensive. He even seemed inclined to be social.

"Traveled fur to-day?" he inquired.

"About thirty miles, as near as I can guess," said Bradley.

"Is that your boy?"

"No, he's no kin to me. We're travelin' together-that's all."

"Goin' to the mines?"

"We are goin' to Murphy's."

"Come from 'Frisco?"

"Yes."

The proprietor of the cabin at this reply fixed his eyes reflectively upon Ben and his companion.

"I'd like to know what he's thinkin' about," said Bradley to himself. "Somehow I mistrust him. A man with that face can't help bein' a scoundrel."

"Don't you find it lonely livin' out here?" he asked.

Jack Carter shrugged his shoulders.

"I don't care for company," he said. "As long as me and the old woman get enough to eat, our own company's good enough for us."

"Are there any mines near-by?" asked Bradley.

"Not very."

"What inducement can he have to live out here in the wilderness?" thought Bradley. "If he were workin' a mine now, I could understand. How does he make a livin', I wonder?"

"Have you lived here long?" he asked.

"Quite a while."

It was clear that Jack did not care to answer definitely, and was disposed to give as little information as possible about himself.

It was yet early when the two travelers felt an inclination to sleep. They had had a hard day's tramp, and wished to be stirring early the next day. As yet, however, they were uncertain whether they would be permitted to sleep in the cabin. Bradley resolved to put the question to the man.

"If you haven't got room for us to sleep," he said, "Ben and I will camp out, as we have done before."

"The old woman's makin' up a bed for you," said Jack. "We don't keep a hotel, but we've got room for you two."

"Thank you."

"Wait here, and I'll see if the bed's ready."

He entered the cabin, probably to consult with his wife.

"I don't know why it is, Ben," said Bradley, in a low voice, "but I mistrust that man."

"Don't you think it safe to sleep here?" asked Ben gravely.

"I think if we are prudent we shall keep a careful watch over our host and hostess; they may mean us harm."

"What motive would they have for harming us, Jake?"

"To get possession of our money. There's a gang of robbers hereabouts, who make their livin' by stopping stages, and lyin' in wait for solitary travelers, and I strongly suspect that this man is one of them."

"Do you judge from his looks?"

"Not wholly, but I can't think of any other motive he can have for livin' in this out-of-the-way place. There are no mines near, and the huntin' wouldn't pay him. I may be mistaken, but that's what I think."

"What shall we do?" asked Ben, a little startled by his companion's suggestion.

"That's more than I can tell you, Ben."

"We might camp out."

"And be surprised in our sleep. No, we shall be as safe in the cabin as outside. Besides, I may be wrong. But, hush! here comes our agreeable friend."

Jack Carter had in his hand a bottle and a tin mug.

"Strangers," said he, "Jack Carter's a poor man, but he's not so poor that he can't offer a glass of wine to a friend."

As he spoke, he poured out a liberal mug of wine and offered it to

Bradley.

Our friend Bradley was not a member of a temperance society, and he could not resist the temptation. His conscience smote him when he thought of the suspicions he had cherished, and there was a sudden revulsion.

"After all," thought he, "Jack Carter is a good fellow. He don't look it, to be sure, but a man can't help his looks What is it the poet says, 'A man may smile and be a villain still.' Jack's a rough customer, but he's treatin' Ben and me tiptop."

"I drink your health, Jack," he said cordially. "You've treated Ben and me like gentlemen, and we're glad to know you. You're the right sort."

And he drained the mug.

Jack Carter filled it again, and passed it to Ben.

"Take a drink, boy," he said. "It will make you feel good."

"No, thank you," said Ben politely.

"What's the matter?" asked Jack, frowning. "Why won't you drink?"

"I never drink," answered Ben. "I promised my father I wouldn't, and

I can't break my word."

"This wine is weak. It wouldn't hurt a baby."

"I would rather not drink," said Ben.

"Ain't you goin' a little too fur, Ben?" remonstrated Bradley. "Your father meant rum and whisky and sich. He wouldn't mind wine."

"Yes, he would," said Ben, resolutely. "I had an uncle who died a drunkard, and it was that that made my father so particular. I promised him faithfully, and now that he's dead, I can't break my work to him."

"The boy's right, Jack," said Bradley. "It won't hurt you and me, but if he don't want to drink, we won't press him."

"It's blasted nonsense!" exclaimed Jack angrily. "The boy's puttin' on airs, that's what's the matter."

"He's a good boy," said Bradley. "You don't know him as well as I do."

"Jest as you say," muttered Jack, in a dissatisfied tone. "If you want to go to bed now, you can."

"I'm ready, for one," said Bradley, rising with, alacrity. "I'm powerful sleepy."

"Come in, then."

They followed their host into the cabin.

CHAPTER XVII.

A TIGHT PLACE.

The lower part of the cabin was divided into two rooms, over which was a loft. There was no staircase; but there was a short ladder by which the ascent was made.

"You're to sleep up there," said Jack, pointing to the loft. "Me and the old woman sleep below."

"All right," said Bradley, gaping. "I can sleep anywhere to-night.

I'm powerful sleepy."

He ascended the ladder first, and Ben followed. There was no bedstead, but a straw pallet was stretched in one corner, with a blanket in place of a quilt.

"I sha'n't undress, Ben," said Bradley, throwing himself down on the rude bed. "I can't keep my eyes open long enough. I think I never felt so sleepy in the whole course of my life."

"I am tired, but not sleepy," returned Ben.

"I won't undress, either. I can sleep just as well in my clothes."

Scarcely a minute had passed when Bradley was breathing in the unconsciousness of slumber.

As Ben lay down beside him, he could not help feeling surprised at his companion's yielding so suddenly to the power of sleep. That he should be tired was not surprising; but when seated outside he had not seemed unusually drowsy, that is, up to the time of his drinking the wine. A quick suspicion flashed upon Ben's mind. Had the wine anything to do with this sudden drowsiness?

Ben had not much experience of life; but he had heard of liquors being drugged, and it seemed possible that the wine which had been offered to Bradley might have been tampered with. If so, it was only too evident what was the object of their host. It was natural to suppose that the two travelers were provided with money, and it was undoubtedly the intention of Jack Carter to rob them in their sleep.

This was not a pleasant thought, nor one calculated to soothe Ben to sleep. He was only a boy, and to find himself in a robber's den was certainly rather a startling discovery. If he had been able to consult with his companion, it would have been a relief; but Bradley was in a profound sleep.

Ben nudged him, but without the slightest effect. He was insensible as a log. Finding more vigorous measures necessary, the boy shook him, but succeeded only in eliciting a few muttered words.

"I can't wake him," thought Ben, more and more disturbed in mind. "I am sure it must be the wine which makes him sleep so heavily. What can I do?"

This question was more easily asked than answered. Ben was quite aware that single-handed he could not cope with a powerful man like Carter. With Bradley's help he would have felt secure; but no assistance could now be expected from his companion. So far as he could see, he must submit to be robbed, and to see his companion robbed. Of course, there was a chance that he might be mistaken. It was possible that Bradley's might be a natural sleep, induced by excessive fatigue, and there might be nothing sinister in the intentions of their host.

Ben, however, found it difficult to convince himself of this, much as he desired to do so. The existence of a gang of robbers in the vicinity, referred to by Bradley, was not calculated to reassure him. If Carter did not belong to this gang, his personal appearance was certainly calculated to foster the suspicion of his connection with them, and the suspicion was strengthened by the fact of his living in this lonely place without any apparent inducement.

For the first time, perhaps, since he had left the East, he wished himself in the security of home. As Deacon Pitkin's hired boy, living on frugal diet, he would have been better off than here at the mercy of a mountain bandit.

But Ben was a boy of spirit, and not inclined to submit in a cowardly manner without first considering if in any possible manner he could guard against the danger which menaced him. Fatigued as he was by the day's ride, he would, under ordinary circumstances, have fallen asleep quickly; but now anxiety and apprehension kept him broad awake.

"If I could only rouse Bradley," he said to himself, "I should feel more comfortable. I don't like the responsibility of deciding what is best to be done."

His thoughts were interrupted by the sound of low voices below. Evidently

Carter and his wife were conversing, and probably about them. Anxious to hear what was said, as this might give him a clue to their plans, Ben rose softly from his low couch, and drew near the edge of the opening through which he had mounted into the loft. In this position he was able to hear what was said.

"They must have money," said Carter. "They would need it to get them out to the mines. Whatever it is, I am bound to have it."

"The man seems strong," replied the wife. "You may not find it an easy task to master him."

"What can he do?" returned Carter contemptuously. "He is in a dead sleep. I put enough stuff into his wine to keep him in a stupor for twelve good hours. If I'm not a match for a sleeping man, I'll go and hang myself."

"But the boy-he took no wine."

"No; he's one of them temperance sneaks. But he's only a baby. I could lay him out with one hand."

"Don't harm him, Jack!" said the woman. "I can't help feeling kindly to him. Our boy, had he lived, would have been about his age. I can't help thinking of that."

"Don't be silly! Because we had a boy once, mustn't interfere with business."

"But you won't hurt him, Jack?" pleaded the woman, who, hard as she seemed, appeared to have a soft side to her nature.

"No; I won't hurt the brat if he behaves himself and doesn't get bumptious. Likely enough he'll be fast asleep. Boys at his age generally sleep well."

"In the morning they will discover that they have been robbed. What will you say to them?"

"Tell them it's none of my business; that I know nothing about it."

"But if the boy is awake, and sees you at work, Jack?"

"Then it will be different. It would have been better for him to have taken the wine."

"Do you think he suspected anything?"

"No; how could he suspect that the wine was drugged? He is one of them temperance sneaks, I tell you."

"How soon are you going up, Jack?"

"In half an hour. I want to give the boy time enough to get asleep.

That will make matters easy."

"Don't you think I had better go up, Jack?"

"Why should you? Why should I let a woman do my work?"

"Then I should know the boy would receive no harm."

"Oh, that's it, is it? You make a great fuss about the boy."

"Yes; I can't help thinking about my own boy."

"Oh, drop that! It makes me sick. Wasn't he my boy as well as yours? I'm sorry he's gone. I could have brought him up to be a help to us in our business."

"Never, Jack, never!" exclaimed his wife fervently.

"Hello! what's that?"

"I mean that I should have been unwilling to have our son grow up no better than we are. He, at any rate, should have been a good man."

"What's up now, old woman? You haven't been attending Sunday-school lately, have you?" demanded Jack, with a sneer.

"I did once, Jack, and I haven't quite forgotten what I learned there, though it don't look like it now."

"Are you going back on me?" demanded Jack fiercely.

"No, Jack, it's too late for that. I have helped you, and I mean to help you, but to-night the sight of that boy, and the thought of our son, who died so long ago, have given me a turn. If it was a man, it would be different. But you have promised you won't harm him, and no more need be said."

"Too much has been said already, to my thinkin'," growled Jack.

"However, that's over, and I expect you to help me if I need help."

Ben heard every word that was said, and it confirmed his suspicions. There was no doubt that an attempt would be made to rob him and his companion before morning, and the prospect was not pleasant. By submitting quietly he would come to no harm, and the loss of the money would not be irreparable. He and Bradley had each started with a hundred dollars, supplied by Miss Doughlas, and thus far but little of this sum had been spent. Their employer would doubtless send them a further supply if they were robbed, but they would be reluctant to apply to her, since the loss would be partly the result of their imprudence.

Ben felt that he was in a tight place, and he was not quite certain what he should or could do.

CHAPTER XVIII.

AN EVENING CALL.

To lie awake in momentary expectation of a hostile attack, from which there is apparently no escape, is by no means a comfortable position. The cabin was in the heart of the woods, with no other dwelling within twenty miles, so far as Ben knew. In fact, if it were true, as Jack had said, that there were no mines near at hand, there were probably no neighbors, except, possibly, of Jack's kind.

The question recurred to Ben: Was he willing to surrender his money, and go forth penniless, or should he attempt to escape or resist?

"If Jake would only wake up!" he thought, surveying, with perplexity, the recumbent form at his side.

But Jake was as senseless as a log, and the attempt to rouse him would inevitably attract attention below and precipitate the attack, besides leaving them utterly penniless.

There was another idea which occurred to our hero: Could he secrete his own money and Jake's, or the greater part of it, and thus save it from the clutches of his dishonest host?

If it had been in the form of bank-bills, there might have been some chance of doing this, but it was not so easy to conceal gold pieces. While considering this question, Ben rose softly and looked out of the window. Strictly speaking, there was no window, but a hole about fifteen inches square, screened by a curtain of coarse cotton cloth. This Ben moved aside, and looked out.

It was not a very dark night. In the half-light Ben was able to see a considerable distance. The height of the opening from the ground was probably not much over twelve feet, as well as the boy could estimate. There would have been no difficulty in his getting out and swinging to the ground, but to this move there were two objections: First, he would be sure to be heard by his enemy below; and, secondly, he was unwilling to leave Jake in the power of the enemy.

While he was standing at the window he heard the noise of some one moving below. The heavy step convinced him that it was Jack. He could not leave his place and lie down without being detected, and he hastily decided to remain where he was.

In this way he might possibly gain time.

Jack softly stepped from round to round of the ladder, and presently his head peered above the floor. He started angrily when he saw the boy at the window.

"What are you about there, boy?" he demanded roughly.

Ben turned, and said composedly: "I am looking out."

"Why are you not in bed and asleep, like your friend?"

"I tried to sleep, sir, but I couldn't."

"Do you expect to get to sleep looking out of that hole?"

"I thought I'd see how light it was."

"Well, I can't have you trampin' round, keepin' the old woman and me awake. I wouldn't have let you sleep here ef I had known that's the way you spend the night."

"I beg pardon if I disturbed you," said Ben politely.

"Well, that don't do no good, your apologizin'. Jest lay down and get to sleep in a hurry, or I'll know the reason why."

"All right, sir," said Ben submissively.

"What's the name of that chap that's with you?" continued Jack.

"It's Jake Bradley."

"He's a sensible man, he is. He lays down and goes to sleep, while you're trampin' round the room and lookin' out of doors. You won't see nothin' to pay you."

"I think you're right, sir. I'll lie down and go to sleep."

"You'd better. Me and the old woman can't be kept awake all night."

When Ben had resumed his place on the floor, the intruder descended the ladder. Though it would have been easy enough to execute his plan of robbery now, he evidently preferred to wait till both the travelers should be asleep.

It was not true, as he had said, that he had heard Ben moving about. In fact, it had been a surprise to him to find the boy up, but this afforded a convenient and plausible pretext for his intrusion, and he had availed himself of it.

CHAPTER XIX.

BEN'S MIDNIGHT EXCURSION.

When Jack Carter went downstairs it was his intention to wait from half an hour to an hour, and then to make another visit to his lodgers. This would allow time for Ben to fall asleep, and, although Jack would have had no difficulty in overcoming his resistance, he preferred to commit the robbery when both the travelers were in a state of unconsciousness.

But he overestimated his ability to keep awake. Usually he was a sound sleeper, and during the day preceding he had taken a long walk across the mountains. The natural result followed. While he was waiting for Ben to fall asleep, he fell asleep himself. Ben was not long in ascertaining this welcome fact. A series of noises, not very musical, announced that Jack was asleep. He had a confirmed habit of snoring, to which, fortunately, his wife had become accustomed, so that it did not disturb her rest.

Ben crept near the edge of the loft and looked over. The bed on which his amiable host reposed was in full view. Both husband and wife were fast asleep, and their sleep was likely to be protracted.

Under this change of circumstances, what was Ben to do?

This was the question which he anxiously asked himself.

Now there would be no difficulty in escaping, if he saw fit. But here there was a difficulty. Jake could not be roused, and, if he could, it would not be very agreeable to lose a night's sleep, for Ben, as well as his host, felt very sleepy. Yet if he allowed himself to remain in the loft, the danger of robbery would recur in the morning, for Jack would be sure to wake earlier than Bradley, who had been drugged, as Ben was convinced.

Sometimes, in the midst of perplexity, a way of relief is suddenly opened. A lucky suggestion, sent, perhaps, by an overruling Providence, provides a path of escape from some menacing evil. This happened in the present instance.

"Why," thought Ben, "can't I take our money, steal downstairs and out of the cabin, and hide it in some secure place where we can find it in the morning? Then I can sleep in security for the remainder of the night, and my thievish friend will be disappointed."

No sooner did the idea occur to Ben than he prepared to carry it out.

As has already been said, Bradley had about a hundred dollars in gold pieces, and Ben as much more. This would have made a very good haul for Jack, who did not anticipate obtaining so much. It was more than our young hero felt willing to lose, and he was prepared to run a large risk in the effort to save it.

The risk, of course, was that he might wake Jack or his wife in coming downstairs. There would be no difficulty in opening the door, for it was not fastened in any way. As to the danger of rousing his entertainers, Ben was not much afraid of waking Jack, for he was evidently in a sound sleep. His wife was more likely to be disturbed, and, in that case, Ben was provided with an excuse. He would say that he was thirsty, and in search of some water, which would have been true enough, though this was not the main object of his expedition.

Ben had not taken off his shoes and stockings, and began to descend the ladder with his shoes on, but it occurred to him that his steps might be audible, and he quietly removed both shoes and stockings. He had previously taken Bradley's money, with the exception of a few dollars, without in the least arousing his sleepy comrade, who, in consequence of the potion he had unsuspiciously taken, was still wrapped in unconscious slumber.

"Now," thought Ben, "I must do my work as quickly as I can."

He was not insensible to the risk he ran, and it was not without a thrill of excitement that he set foot on the floor of the cabin, and looked at the sleeping faces of Jack Carter and his wife. But there was no time to waste. He stepped softly to the door and opened it.

Just then the woman stirred in her sleep, and uttered something unintelligible. Ben was alarmed lest she were about to wake up, and stood stock-still, with his fingers on the latch. But there was no further sound. The woman partially turned over, and soon her quiet, regular breathing notified Ben that sleep had resumed its power over her. Probably she had stirred in consequence of some uneasy dream.

With a deep breath of relief, Ben opened the door, passed out, and closed it softly after him.

He was out of the house, and in the freedom of the woods. Before morning he might have put fifteen miles between him and the cabin of his foes. He would have felt disposed to do so, and avoid all further trouble, if Bradley had been with him, and in condition to travel. As this was not to be thought of, he proceeded to search for a suitable place to secrete his troublesome treasure.

The cabin stood in a valley, or canon, in the shadow of gigantic pine-trees, rising straight as a flagpole to the altitude of nearly two hundred feet. They were forest giants, impressive in their lofty stature, and Ben regarded them with wonder and awe. They were much smaller in every way than the so-called big trees to be found in the Calaveras and Mariposa groves; but these had not at that time been discovered, and the pines were the largest trees our hero had ever encountered.

Ben looked about him in vain to find a suitable hiding-place in the immediate neighborhood of the cabin. If there had been a large flat rock under which he could have placed the gold pieces, that would have suited him; but there was absolutely nothing of the kind in sight.

So Ben wandered away, hardly knowing whither his steps were carrying him, till he must have been at least a quarter of a mile distant from the cabin.

Here his attention was attracted by a tree of larger circumference than any he had seen nearer, which showed the ravages of time. The bark was partly worn away, and, approaching nearer, Ben saw that it had begun to decay from within. There was an aperture about a foot above the ground through which he could readily thrust his hand.

"That's the very thing!" exclaimed Ben, his eyes lighting up with pleasure. "Nobody would ever think of looking for money there. Here I can hide our gold, and to-morrow, when we set out on our journey, we can take this tree on our way."

Ben took from his pockets the gold which belonged to Bradley and himself, and wrapping them securely in a paper which he happened to have with him, he thrust the whole into the cavity in the tree.

"There!" said he, "our treasure is much safer there than it would be in our possession, for to-night, at least."

Ben carefully took the bearings of the tree, that he might not forget it. There was little difficulty about this, as it was larger than any of its neighbors, not so tall, perhaps, but of greater circumference.

"I shall remember it now," he said to himself.

As Ben walked back to the humble cabin he became very drowsy. He was quite fatigued with his day's march, and it was now nearly or quite two hours since his companion had fallen asleep.

It was fortunate for him that Ben had been more wakeful.

"I shall be glad enough to sleep now," thought Ben. "I don't know when I have felt more tired."

He reached the cabin door, and listened outside to learn whether any one were stirring. He could still hear the sonorous snore of Jack, and could distinguish the deep breathing of his hostess. All seemed to be safe.

He softly opened the door, and closed it after him. Without arousing any one, he made his way up the ladder to the loft, where Bradley lay precisely as he had left him.

Ben threw himself down beside him with a deep sigh of satisfaction, and in ten minutes he, too, was sound asleep.

CHAPTER XX.

A THIEF'S DISAPPOINTMENT.

Jack Garter, regardless of his plans respecting his guests, slept through the night, and it was not till after the sun rose that he opened his eyes. His wife was already up and moving about the room.

Jack stretched himself negligently, but all at once his purpose flashed upon him.

"Bess, what time is it?" he demanded.

"Past six o'clock, as you can see by the sun."

"Curse it! what made me fall asleep?" ejaculated Jack, with an oath.

"Now it may be too late."

"How long have you been awake, Bess?" he asked.

"An hour or more."

"Why didn't you wake me up?" demanded Jack sharply.

"I didn't know you wanted me to," answered his wife. "Only yesterday you swore at me for waking you up an hour later."

"Yesterday isn't to-day, and I had something to do," said Jack, looking significantly upward.

"Didn't you attend to it last night?"

"No; curse my drowsiness! I fell asleep like a natural-born fool that I was."

"How could I know that? I was asleep myself."

"You always have some excuse," said Jack, rather unreasonably. "Just quit movin' round and makin' a noise. It may not be too late yet."

No sound was heard in the loft above. Happily, the two lodgers might still be asleep, so Jack said to himself, and in that case he might still be able to carry out his plan. At any rate, there was no time to lose, and he began softly to ascend the ladder.

When his head reached the level of the flooring he looked eagerly at the rude couch where his guests lay. Both were fast asleep. Bradley was still held in the power of the powerful drug which had been mingled with his wine, and Ben had yielded to the sound and healthful slumber which at his age follows fatigue. His boyish face lay on his hand, and he looked innocent and happy. There was a smile about his lips, for he was dreaming of his far-away home.

The sight might have appealed to any one less hardened than Jack Carter, calling up memories of his own dead boy, and powerfully appealing to what heart he had left. But Jack felt simply relieved to find that the boy, whose wakefulness he had feared, was sound asleep.

"All the better," he muttered. "It isn't too late, after all. Now,

Jack Carter, is your time. I hope you'll make a good haul."

Treading softly, Jack stepped to the side of Bradley. He thought it best to rid him first, for there was no danger of his waking up.

But he was destined to disappointment. The most thorough search brought to light only five dollars in gold.

"What has he done with his money?" muttered the thief, with a frown.

"Of course, he must have more."

The idea came to him that the bulk of the money might have been given to the boy, who was less likely to attract the notice of plunderers. This was a point easily settled, and Jack turned his attention to Ben.

Ben was asleep when the search commenced, but his sleep was not as profound as Bradley's, and he woke up. But, luckily, recollection came with consciousness, and summoning all his self-command, he counterfeited sleep, not interfering with Jack or his designs. He was willing to lose the little he had in his pocket, and, besides, he was curious to hear what Jack would say when he found out how inconsiderable was the booty which he secured.

It must be admitted that Ben found it difficult to restrain himself from some movement which would have betrayed to the thief that he was awake. Jack, however, being fully convinced that Ben was asleep, did not fix his eyes upon the countenance of his young lodger, and so remained ignorant of his wakefulness.

The second search proved no more satisfactory than the first. The boy was no richer than the man.

In a low voice Jack indulged in an oath indicating his deep disgust.

"I didn't think they were such poor tramps," he said to himself, "or I wouldn't have taken all this trouble. Only ten dollars between the two of them! Why, they're little more than beggars?"

Stay! They might have concealed their money. There was no place in the loft, for it was wholly bare of furniture, but their luggage was thrown down carelessly. There were no lodes, and Jack was able to extend his search to their knapsacks; but he found nothing that repaid him. He was forced finally to the conclusion that they were as poor as they seemed.

Had Jack Carter been one of those generous highwaymen, of whom we sometimes read, he would have disdained to rob Ben and his friend of their little all. But indeed that was not his style.

He coolly pocketed the two gold pieces, which were all he had been able to find, and sullenly descended the ladder.

His wife looked at him inquiringly.

"Look at that!" he said grumblingly, as he displayed the two gold pieces.

"Was it all you could find?"

"Yes."

"They must be poor."

"Poor! They are beggars."

The woman, who was not as hard as she looked, was struck with compassion.

"Give it back to them, Jack," she entreated. "It is little enough, and they will have need of it."

"So do I have need of it," growled her lord and master.

"No, you don't, Jack. It isn't worth your taking."

"I'm the best judge of that, woman."

"They will suffer. I can't bear to have that boy suffer. He reminds me so of our dead son."

"You're a fool!" said her husband roughly.

"And you have no heart!" said his wife bitterly.

"I don't want one if it's going to make a fool of me. Come, hurry up the breakfast, for I must be out of the way before they come down. They'll miss their money, and I don't want to be asked any questions."

"What shall I say if they ask me where it is, Jack?"

"Anything you like," he answered impatiently. "Say the cat did it, or anything else. Do you think a woman needs teachin' what she is to say?"

"They will think we did it," persisted his wife.

"Let them. They can't prove anything. Just hurry up that breakfast,

I tell you."

The wife did as she was ordered, and Jack sat down to his breakfast. He ate heartily, having a conscience that did not trouble him about such trifles as plundering the guests who had slept beneath his roof, and rose to leave the house.

"Give 'em some breakfast," he said, as he opened the door; "and tell 'em you won't take no pay on account of their loss. That'll about make things square, I reckon. I've taken my pay in advance."

He shouldered his gun and went out into the woods.

CHAPTER XXI.

BEN'S SAVINGS-BANK.

It was not till an hour afterward that Ben rose from his lowly couch, and, by dint of violent shaking, succeeded in rousing Bradley.

"Come, Bradley, wake up!" he cried. "The sun is high, and it is time we were on our way."

Bradley stretched himself, took a long breath, and said:

"I must have had a long sleep."

"Yes, you dropped off as soon as you lay down, and have slept ever since."

"And did you sleep as soundly?"

"No, I was awake twice during the night," answered Ben.

"I don't know how it is, but I am sleepy still. Seems to me I don't stand fatigue as well as you. I am sleepy yet, and feel as if I could sleep all the forenoon."

"The effects of the drug," thought Ben.

Ben considered whether he should tell Bradley what had happened during the night. He decided briefly to say a few words about it in a whisper, and postpone a full explanation till later, for their hostess was below, and could hear any loud word that might be uttered. Bradley was instructed that he must claim to have lost five dollars.

"But I had a hundred," said Bradley, feeling in his pockets.

"It's all right," whispered Ben. "I'll explain by and by. Not a word of the loss till after breakfast."

Bradley was quite bewildered, and utterly failed to understand the situation. But he had considerable faith in his young companion, and was willing to follow Ben's instructions. They descended the ladder, Ben in advance.

The woman looked at them sharply, to see if they had yet discovered the robbery, but each seemed unconcerned.

"They don't know it yet," she said to herself.

"Madam, can you give us some breakfast?" asked Ben politely.

"I'll give you such as I have," said Mrs. Carter, feeling a little remorse for her husband's theft, and pity for what she supposed their penniless condition.

"That will be perfectly satisfactory, and we shall be much obliged to you."

The breakfast was nearly ready in anticipation of their needs, and they partook of it heartily.

Now came the critical moment.

Ben thrust his hand into his pocket, appearing to search for his money, and, after a brief space, withdrew it in apparent dismay.

"I can't find my money," he said.

Mrs. Carter's face flushed, but she said nothing. She anticipated their suspicion, and was ashamed.

"Bradley," said Ben, "have you your money?"

Jake Bradley repeated the search, and he, too, expressed surprise.

"I had it when I went to bed," he added.

"What is it?" asked the woman slowly, turning to them a troubled face. "Have you lost anything?"

"I don't seem to find my money, ma'am," answered Bradley.

"Nor I mine," said Ben. "It's curious."

Mrs. Carter could not tell by their manner whether they suspected anything, but she had her story ready. It was an invention, but life with Jack Carter had left her few compunctions about such a simple matter as telling a lie.

"I missed something myself," she said. "We don't lock our door of nights, and I reckon some tramp got in last night, when we were asleep, and robbed us all. Have you lost much, you two?"

"Not much, ma'am. There wasn't much to take."

"It's a pity. I am sorry it happened under my roof. But we slept very sound last night, Jack and me, and that's the way it must have come."

She looked at them critically, to detect, if she could, whether they suspected her husband or herself, but both the travelers were on their guard.

"Did you have much taken, ma'am?" asked Bradley.

"No," she answered hurriedly, rather ashamed of the imposture. "We ain't rich, Jack nor I."

"What I am most sorry for," said Ben, "is that we have nothing to pay for our accommodations."

"You're welcome to your lodging and what you've ate," said the woman sincerely. "And, if you like, I'll put up some luncheon for you to eat by and by."

"Thank you, ma'am, it will be very acceptable," answered Bradley.

"She's better than her husband," thought Ben.

"After all, we haven't lost much, for we shall get nearly the worth of our lost money."

The woman remarked, with some surprise, that they did not take their loss much to heart.

"How do you expect to get along without money?" she could not help asking.

"We're used to roughing it, ma'am," said Bradley. "I'm an old miner, and I think I can find some of my old chums before long."

By this time luncheon was ready, and they soon left the cabin.

Bradley could no longer repress his curiosity.

"Now, Ben, tell me all about it," he said. "Where is our money?"

Ben looked back, to make sure that he would not be overheard, and answered: "I put it in the bank for security, Jake."

"What do you mean?"

"If I am not very much mistaken, we shall find it hidden in a hole in a tree, quarter of a mile away."

"Who put it there?" asked his companion, in surprise.

"I did."

"When?"

"Last night, about midnight, as near as I can guess."

Ben laughed at his companion's evident perplexity, and told him in detail the story of the night's adventure.

"Ben, I'm proud of you," said Bradley, slapping our hero on the back. "There are not many grown men that would have known what to do under the circumstances."

"I confess that I was very much puzzled myself," said Ben modestly.

"I could have done nothing if our honest host hadn't fallen asleep."

"He would feel rather provoked if he knew that nearly all of our money is untouched," said Bradley; "that is, if we find it again."

"There's no fear of that," said Ben. "Do you see that tree yonder?"

"The large one?"

"Yes."

"That is my savings-bank."

They quickened their steps till they reached the stately monarch of the forest. Ben quickly thrust his hand into the cavity and drew out the precious parcel which he had committed to it during the night. It was precisely as he had placed it there. No one had touched it.

"Now," said Ben, "I will give you ninety-five dollars. That is the amount of which I picked your pocket last night."

"You are a pickpocket of the right sort," said his companion. "You took my money in order to save it."

Their money recovered, they started on their day's march, and nightfall found them twenty miles nearer their destination.

CHAPTER XXII.
THE ARRIVAL AT MURPHY'S.

One morning about eleven o'clock they came in sight of Murphy's. It was only a mining-settlement of the most primitive description. A few tents and cabins, with rough, bearded men scattered here and there, intent upon working their claims, gave it a picturesque appearance, which it has lost now. It was then a more important place than at present, however, for the surface diggings are exhausted, and it is best known-to-day by its vicinity to the famous Calaveras grove of big trees.

"So this is Murphy's?" said Ben, rather disappointed. "It doesn't seem to be much of a place."

"You didn't expect to see a regular town, did you?" asked Bradley.

"I don't know. I hardly knew what to expect. It seems a rough place."

"And I suppose the people seem rough, too?"

"Yes."

"So they are in appearance; but you can't tell what a man has been, by his looks here. Why, the man that worked the next claim to me was a college graduate, and not far away was another who had been mayor of a Western city."

"And were they dressed like these men here?" asked Ben.

"Quite as roughly. It won't do to wear store-clothes at the mines."

"No, I suppose not; but these men look like immigrants just come over."

Bradley laughed.

"Wait till we have been at work a little while, and we shall look no better," he said, laughing.

"What is that?" asked Ben suddenly, stopping short while an expression of horror came over his face.

Bradley followed the direction of his finger, and saw suspended from a tree the inanimate body of a man, the features livid and distorted, and wearing an expression of terror and dismay, as if his fate had come upon him without time for preparation.

"I reckon that's a thief," answered Bradley unconcernedly.

"A thief! Do they hang people for stealing out here?"

"Yes, they have to. You see, my lad, there ain't any laws here, nor courts. If a man steals, the miners just take the matter into their own hands, and if there ain't a doubt of it, they hang him as soon as they catch him."

"It's horrible!" said Ben, who had never before seen the victim of a violent death.

"Maybe it is, but what can we do?"

"Put him in prison," suggested Ben.

"There ain't any prisons, and, if there were, there would be nobody to keep them."

Just then Bradley was hailed by a rough-looking man, whom at home

Ben would have taken for a tramp.

"What, Bradley, back again? I didn't expect to see you here?"

"I didn't expect to come, Hunter, but I fooled away my money in

'Frisco, and have come back for more."

"And who's this boy-your son, or nephew?"

"No; he's no kin to me. I ran across him down to 'Frisco. Ben, let me make you acquainted with my old chum, Frank Hunter. He isn't much to look at, but-"

"I have seen better days," interrupted Hunter, smiling. "I was rather a dandy in my college days at old Yale, though I don't look like it now."

Ben regarded him with surprise. He had not dreamed that this sun-brown, bearded man, in the roughest of mining-garbs, had ever seen the inside of a college.

Hunter smiled at the boy's evident surprise.

"I don't look like a college graduate, do I? But I assure you I am not the worst-dressed man in camp. My friend, the mayor, is rougher-looking than I. Some time I hope to return to the haunts of civilization, and then I will try to conform to habits which I have almost forgotten."

"How are you making out, Hunter?" asked Bradley.

"Pretty well. I have made more here in six months than I did by three years' practise of law before I came out here."

"Do you like it as well, Mr. Hunter?" Ben could not help asking curiously.

"No, I don't; but then, it's only for a time, as I say to myself when I get tired of the rough life I am leading. When I've made a respectable pile I shall start for 'Frisco, and take passage home, put up my shingle again, and wait for clients with money enough to pay my board while I'm waiting. A young lawyer needs that always."

"Perhaps you'll be Judge Hunter, in time," said Bradley.

"I've served in that capacity already," said Hunter unexpectedly, "and that not longer ago than yesterday. Do you see that poor wretch up there?" and he pointed to the suspended body already referred to.

"Yes; what did he do?"

"He was a notorious thief-served a term in the penitentiary East for stealing, and came out here to practise his profession. But this climate is unhealthy for gentlemen in that line of business."

"Did he rob anybody here?"

"Yes; you remember Johnson?"

"Is he still here?"

"He is about ready to go home, with money enough to lift the mortgage from his farm. We all knew it, for Johnson was so happy that he took everybody into his confidence. He had all his money tied up in a bag which he kept in his tent.

"Imprudent, of course, but we haven't any banks or safes here," added Hunter, meeting the question in Ben's eyes. "Well, this rascal, Ross, wormed himself into his confidence, found out exactly where the bag was kept, and night before last, in the middle of the night, he crept to the tent, and was in the act of carrying off the bag, when, as luck would have it, my friend, the mayor, who was taking a night walk in the hope of curing a severe headache, came upon him.

"Ross showed fight, but was overpowered, and tied securely till morning. When morning came we tried him, I being judge. He was found guilty, and sentenced to be hung. The sentence was carried into effect in the afternoon. He won't steal any more, I reckon."

Ben took another hasty look at the dangling criminal whose end had been so sudden and horrible, and he shuddered.

"Why don't you take him down?" he asked.

"It was ordered that he hang for twenty-four hours, as a warning to any others in camp who might be tempted to steal. The time isn't up yet.

"You are a young gold-hunter," said Hunter, scanning over hero's youthful face.

"Yes, I am," Ben confessed; "but I had to earn a living, and I thought I could do it better here than at home."

"Are you from the East?"

"I am from Hampton, in New York State."

"I know something of Hampton," said Hunter. "I have never been there; but I have a distant relative living there."

"Who is it?" asked Ben, with interest. "I know everybody there."

"I dare say you know my relative, for I am given to understand that he is the great man of Hampton."

"Mayor Sturgis?"

"Yes, that is his name. He married a cousin of my mother, so the relationship is not very close. He is rich, isn't he?"

"He is the richest man in Hampton."

"I suppose he is aware of that fact," said Hunter, laughing.

"If he isn't, his son, Sam, is," replied Ben. "Sam wanted to engage me as his servant before I came away. He wanted me to black his boots."

"And you objected, I suppose?"

"I wouldn't work for Sam Sturgis for a hundred dollars a month!" said Ben emphatically.

"Then you don't like him?"

"He is very big-feeling," said Ben, using a boy's word, "and likes to boss all the rest of the boys. He thinks he is far above us all."

"He ought to come out here. California takes the airs out of a man if he has any. We are all on an equality here, and the best man wins-I mean the man of the most pluck-for success doesn't depend on moral excellence exactly. Well, old friend, are you going to settle down among us again?"

It was to Bradley this question was addressed.

"I don't know. I'm here on a little matter of business, along of this boy. Is Richard Dewey here now?"

"Dewey? No. He had poor luck, and he dusted a month ago."

Ben and his companion exchanged glances of disappointment.

"Where did he go?" asked Bradley, who was evidently getting discouraged.

"He was going to the mountains," he said. "He had been studying up something about minerals, and he had an idea that he'd find a rich ledge among the Sierras that would pay better than this surface-mining."

"Is there anybody that knows what direction he took?"

"My friend, the mayor, knows as well as any man. Dewey was his next neighbor, and often talked over his plans with him."

"Then we will go and see the mayor."

"No need of going, here he comes."

CHAPTER XXIII.
AMONG THE SIERRAS.

Ben had heard of mayors, and once he had seen one, a pompous-looking man who had once served in that capacity in an inland city of some twenty thousand inhabitants, and he supposed that all mayors were alike. He could hardly believe his eyes, therefore, when he saw before him a man of medium height, dressed in a ragged shirt and trousers, and wearing a hat once white, but now dirt-begrimed.

"Friends of yours, judge?" said the newcomer, speaking to Hunter, and indicating by a nod Ben and his companion.

"You ought to know one of them, mayor," said Hunter.

"Why, it's Bradley," said the mayor, extending his hand cordially.

"Glad to see you back again."

Bradley shook hands, and introduced Ben.

"I'm told you can tell me where to find Richard Dewey, colonel," said

Bradley, employing another title of the mayor.

"I can't just say where he is," said the mayor; "but I can tell you where he meant to go."

"That will help us."

"You don't mean him any harm?" asked the mayor quickly.

"Far from it. We have the best news for him."

"Because Dick Dewey is a friend of mine, and I wouldn't bring him into trouble for the richest claim in Californy."

"That's where we agree, colonel. The fact is, there's a young lady in 'Frisco who has come out on purpose to find him-his sweetheart, and an heiress, at that. Me and Ben have agreed to find him for her, and that's the long and short of it."

"Then I'm with you, Bradley. I've seen the girl's picture. Dick showed it to me one day, and she does credit to his taste. He's had bad luck at the mines; but-"

"That won't matter when them two meet," said Bradley. "She's better than any claim he can find this side the mountains."

Bradley and our young hero spent the remainder of the day and the night at Murphy's, hospitably provided for by the judge and the mayor, and Ben listened with avidity to the stories of the miners and their varying luck. If he had not been in search of Richard Dewey, he would have tarried at Murphy's, selected a claim, and gone to work the very next day. He was anxious to have his share in the rough but fascinating life which these men were leading. To him it seemed like a constant picnic, with the prospect of drawing a golden prize any day, provided you attended to business.

"That will come by and by," he thought to himself. "We must find

Cousin Ida's beau, and then we can attend to business."

Somehow, it seemed more natural to use the first name by which he had known the young lady who employed him than the real name which he had learned later. It may be necessary to remind the reader that her name was Florence Douglas.

The next morning, after breakfast, the two friends left Murphy's, and bent their course toward the mountains where they were told that Richard Dewey was likely to be found. The direction given them was, it must be confessed, not very definite, and the chances seemed very much against their succeeding in the object of their search.

A week later we will look in upon them toward nightfall. They were among the mountains now.

After the close of a laborious day they had tethered their animals to a tree, and were considering a very important subject, namely, where to find anything that would serve for supper. Their supply of provisions was exhausted, and there was no means of purchasing a fresh supply.

Bradley took out his supply of gold, and surveyed it ruefully.

"Ben," said he, "I never knew before how little good there is in bein' rich. Here we've both got money, and we can't get anything for it. It's cheap traveling for we haven't spent anything sence we've left Murphy's."

"I wish we could spend some of our money," said Ben uneasily. "If there was only a baker's, or an eating-house here, I'd be willing to pay five dollars for a good square meal."

"So would I. Somehow, gold don't look as good to me as it used to.

We may starve to death with money in our pockets."

Ben's eyes were fixed upon a slender brook not far away that threaded its silvery way down a gentle incline from the midst of underbrush.

"I wonder if we can't catch some trout," he said. "Don't they have trout in these mountains?"

"To be sure they do; and the best in the world," said Bradley briskly. "The California mountain trout can't be beat."

"But we have no fishing-tackle," suggested Ben.

"Never mind, we have our guns."

"How will that help us?"

"We can shoot them, to be sure."

Ben looked surprised.

"Didn't you ever shoot pickerel? We can shoot trout in the same way. Come, Ben, follow me, and we'll see if we can't have a good supper, after all."

Leaving their mustangs to gather a supper from the scanty herbage in their neighborhood, the two friends made their way to the brook. It had seemed very near, but proved to be fully a quarter of a mile away. When they reached it they brought their guns into requisition, and soon obtained an appetizing mess of trout, which only needed the service of fire to make a meal fit for an epicure.

"I can hardly wait to have them cooked," sard Ben. "I'm as hungry as a hunter. I understand what that means now."

"I sha'n't have any trouble in keeping up with you, Ben," said his companion. "We'll have a supper fit for a king."

They gathered some dry sticks, and soon a fire was blazing, which, in the cool night air, sent out a welcome heat.

After supper they lay down on their backs and looked up into the darkening sky. Ben felt that it was a strange situation. They were in the heart of the Sierras, miles, perhaps many miles, away from any human being, thousands of miles away from the quiet village where Ben had first seen the light. Yet he did not feel disturbed or alarmed. His wanderings had inspired self-reliance, and he did not allow himself to be troubled with anxious cares about the future. If by a wish he could have been conveyed back to his uncle's house in the far East, he would have declined to avail himself of the privilege. He had started out to make a living for himself, and he was satisfied that if he persevered he would succeed in the end.

"What are you thinking about, Ben?" asked Bradley, after a long pause.

"I was thinking how strange it seems to be out here among the mountains," answered Ben, still gazing on the scenery around him.

"I don't see anything strange about it," said his less imaginative comrade. "Seein' we came here on our horses, it would be strange to be anywhere else."

"I mean it is strange to think we are so far away from everybody."

"I don't foller you, Ben. I suppose it's sorter lonelylike, but that ain't new to me."

"I never realized how big the world was when I lived at home," said Ben, in a slow, thoughtful way.

"Yes, it's a pretty largish place, that's a fact."

"What were you thinking of, Jake?" asked Ben, in his turn.

"I was thinkin' of two things: whereabouts Dewey has managed to hide himself, and then it occurred to me how consolin' it would be to me if I could light on a pound of smokin'-tobacco. I've got a pipe, but it ain't no good without tobacco."

"That don't trouble me much, Jake," said Ben, with a smile.

"It's the next thing to a good supper, Ben," said Bradley; "but I might as well wish for the moon."

"You needn't wish in vain for that," said Ben, pointing out the orb of evening, with its pale-yellow light peeping over the tall tree-tops, and irradiating the scene with its pensive shimmer.

"I can see it, but that don't help me any," said Bradley. "If I saw a world made of tobacco up in yonder sky, it would only make me feel worse because I couldn't get any."

"What was it you was a-wishin' for, friend?" asked an unfamiliar voice.

Bradley sprang to his feet, and Ben followed suit.

They saw two strange figures, clad in Spanish style, with large, napping sombreros on their heads, who unheard, had descended the mountains, and were now close upon them.

"Who are you?" asked Bradley doubtfully.

"Friends," was the reassuring reply. "We'll join your little party if you have no objection. I'd invite you to take a drink if there was any saloon handy. As there isn't, jest help yourself to this," and he drew out a pouch of smoking-tobacco.

"Just what I was wantin'," said Bradley, delighted. "You're welcome, whoever you are."

"Ben, can't you get together some sticks and light the fire? It's coolish."

CHAPTER XXIV.

BEATEN AT HIS OWN GAME.

Bradley was of a social disposition, and even without the gift of tobacco would have been glad of an addition to their small party.

"I'm glad to see you," he said, repeating his welcome. "I wonder I didn't hear you comin'. Have you been long in Californy?"

"Well onto a year," said the one who seemed the elder of the two.

"How is it with you, stranger?"

"I have been here about as long," answered Bradley. "Ben has only just come out."

"What luck have you had?" pursued the questioner.

"Good and bad. I made quite a pile, and went to 'Frisco and gambled it away like a fool. Now I've come back for another trial."

'"What might your name be?"

"Bradley-Jake Bradley. It isn't much of a name, but it'll do for me.

The boy is Ben Stanton—come from the East."

"My name is Bill Mosely," said the other. "My friend's Tom Hadley. We're both from Missouri, and, though I say it, we're about as wide-awake as they make 'em. We don't stand no back talk, Tom and me. When a man insults me, I drop him," and the speaker rolled his eyes in what was meant to stimulate ferocity.

Bradley eyed him shrewdly, and was not quite so much impressed as Mosely intended him to be. He had observed that the greatest boasters did not always possess the largest share of courage.

"Isn't that so, Tom?" asked Bill Mosely, appealing to his friend.

"I should say so," answered Tom, nodding emphatically.

"You've seen me in a scrimmage more than once?"

"I should say I have."

"Did you ever see me shoot a man that riled me?"

"Dozens of times," returned Hadley, who appeared to play second fiddle to his terrible companion.

"That's the kind of man I am," said Bill Mosely, in a tone of complacency.

Still, Bradley did not seem particularly nervous or frightened. He was fast making up his mind that Mosely was a cheap bully, whose words were more terrible than his deeds. Ben had less experience of men, and he regarded the speaker as a reckless desperado, ready to use his knife or pistol on the least provocation. He began to think he would have preferred solitude to such society. He was rather surprised to hear Bradley say quietly:

"Mosely, you're a man after my own heart. That's the kind of man I be. If a man don't treat me right, I shoot him in his tracks. One day I was drinkin' in a saloon among the foothills, when I saw a man winkin' at me. I waited to see if he would do it again. When he did, I hauled out my revolver and shot him dead."

"You did?" exclaimed Mosely uneasily.

"Of course I did; but I was rather sorry afterward when I heard that his eyelids were weak and he couldn't help it."

"Did you get into any trouble about it, stranger?" asked Mosely, with a shade of anxiety.

"No; none of the party dared touch me. Besides, I did the handsome thing. I had the man buried, and put a stone over him. I couldn't do any more, could I?"

"No," said Mosely dubiously, and he drew a little farther away from

Bradley.

"What do you find to eat?" he inquired, after a pause. "Tom and I are as hungry as if we hadn't eaten anything for a week. You haven't got any provisions left over?"

"No; but you can have as good a supper as we had, and we had a good one. What do you say to trout, now?"

Bill Mosely smacked his lips.

"Jest show me where I'll find some," he said.

Bradley pointed to the brook from which he had drawn his supply.

"I don't mind helping you," he said. "Ben, are you tired?"

"No, Jake."

"Then come along, and we'll try to get some supper for our friends."

"All right!" said Ben cheerfully.

In a short time a fresh supply of trout was drawn from the brook, and they were roughly cooked at the fire, Bradley officiating as cook.

"Now, my friends, set up," said he. "I'm sorry I can't give you any potatoes, but the barrel's out, and it's too late to get any at the store. Likewise, you must excuse the puddin', as it's too late to make any."

The two visitors appeared to think no apologies were needful, for they made short work with the trout. From the manner in which they devoured their supper, it was quite evident that it was some time since they had eaten. Ben and Bradley did not join them, having already eaten heartily.

"I hope you relished your supper, gentlemen," said Bradley politely.

"I should say we did," responded Tom Hadley.

"I say, them trout beat the world."

"I'll shoot the man that says they don't!" said Bill Mosely, relapsing into his old tone.

"So will I!" exclaimed Bradley, springing to his feet and brandishing his revolver.

Ben began to see that he was playing a part, and, with assumed gravity, he looked to see what effect it would have on their new friend.

"I say, stranger, don't handle that weapon of yours so careless," said Mosely uneasily.

"I guess you're right," said Bradley, appearing to calm down. "Once I was swingin' my gun kinder careless, and it went off and hit my friend, Jim Saunders, in his shoulder. Might have been worse. He had a narrer escape. But Jim couldn't complain. I jest took care of him, night and day, till he got well. I couldn't do any more'n that, now, could I?"

"I reckon he'd rather you hadn't shot him," said Mosely dryly.

"I reckon you're right," said Bradley, with equanimity. "Such little accidents will happen sometimes, Mosely. Somehow, you can't always help it."

"It's best to be keerful," observed Mosely uneasily.

"I should say so," echoed his friend, Tom Hadley.

"Right you both are!" said Bradley affably. "I say, Mosely, I like you. You're jest such a sort of man as I am. You'd jest as lieve shoot a man as to eat your dinner; now, wouldn't you?"

"If he'd insulted me," said Mosely hesitatingly.

"Of course. Come, now, how many men have you killed, first and last?"

"About twenty, I should think," answered the bully, who seemed to grow meeker and more peaceable as Bradley's apparent reckless ferocity increased.

"Only twenty!" exclaimed Bradley contemptuously. "Why, that's nothing at all!"

"How many have you killed?" asked Mosely uneasily.

"Seventy or eighty, I should say," answered Bradley carelessly. "Of course, a man can't keep an account of all these little affairs. I did once think I'd keep a list, but I got tired of it after a short time, and gave it up after I'd got up to forty-seven."

"Where was you raised, stranger?" asked Mosely.

"In Kentucky-glorious old Kentuck! and if there's a man dares to say a word against my State, I'll take his life!" and Bradley sprang to his feet.

"Lay down again, stranger," interposed Bill Mosely hastily. "There's no one here wants to say a word agin' Kentuck. It's a glorious old State, as you say. Isn't it, Tom?"

"I should say so," responded Tom Hadley, using his customary formula.

"Are you in search of gold, Mosely?" asked Bradley, in a more quiet manner.

"We're kinder prospectin' among the hills," answered Mosely.

"You haven't come across anything yet, have you?"

"Not yet. Have you?"

"We're looking for a friend that's gone ahead. Maybe he's struck it rich. When we find him we'll turn in and help him."

"You've got one advantage of us, stranger. You've got hosses, and we've had to walk."

"Why didn't you buy animals?"

"We did, but they were stolen from us a little way back."

"If our hosses should be stolen," said Bradley, "the thieves would die within a week."

Mosely and his friend looked at each other in silence, and the conversation languished.

"Ben," said Bradley, after the two visitors were fast asleep, "shall

I tell you what I think of these two men?"

"Well, Bradley?"

"They are thieves, and they meant to steal our hosses."

"Won't they do it now?"

Bradley laughed.

"They'll be afraid to," he answered. "I've beaten them at their own game, and they think I'm as desperate a bully as they pretend to be. No; they won't think it safe to interfere with our property."

"How many men did you say you had killed, Jake?" asked Ben, with a smile.

"That was all talk. Thank Heaven, I haven't the blood of any fellow creature on my hands!"

CHAPTER XXV.
THE HORSE-THIEVES.

All four slept soundly, but the visitors awoke first.

"Are you awake, Tom?" inquired Mosely.

"I should say so," answered his friend.

Bill Mosely raised himself on his elbow and surveyed Ben and Bradley. Their deep, tranquil breathing showed that they were sound asleep.

Mosely next glanced at the mustangs which were tethered near-by.

"Tom," said he, "I wish we had them mustangs. It's a deal easier ridin' than walkin'."

"I should say so."

"When I struck this party last night I meant to have 'em; but this man is such a bloody ruffian that I don't know as it would be safe."

Hadley said nothing. His customary phrase would not apply, and he was a man of few words, besides.

"What did he say he would do if a fellow stole his horses, Tom?"

"Said he'd die within a week," answered Had-ley, with unfailing memory.

Bill Mosely looked discouraged. He privately thought Bradley was just the man to keep his word, and he did not fancy getting into difficulty with him.

"That depends on whether he caught him," he said, after a while, hopefully.

"I should say so, Bill."

"Now," said Mosely, lowering his voice, "if we could get away while they are asleep, there wouldn't be much chance of their knowin' where we were."

"That's so, Bill."

"Anyway, if we don't take 'em we may be overtaken by the party that we borrowed some gold-dust from."

Tom Hadley responded in his customary manner.

"And that would be mighty bad luck," continued Mosely, with a shudder.

"I should say so, Bill."

In fact, Mosely felt that their situation was not likely to be made worse by a new theft. Only thirty miles away was a party of miners with whom they had worked in company, but without much success, till, emboldened by temptation and opportunity, they had stolen a bag of gold-dust from a successful comrade, and fled under cover of the night.

In the primitive state of society at the mines, stealing was a capital offense, and if they were caught their lives would probably pay the penalty. Even now some of the injured party might be on their track, and this naturally inspired them with uneasiness. Thus they were between two fires, and, in spite of the fear with which Bradley had inspired them, it looked as if another theft would conduce to their safety. If they carried away the mustangs, Bradley and Ben, even if they hit on the right trail, would have to pursue them on foot, and among the Sierras a man is no match for a mustang in speed and endurance.

"I've a great mind to carry off them mustangs," said Mosely thoughtfully. "Are you with me?"

"I should say so."

"Why don't you ever say something else, Tom?" demanded Mosely impatiently.

"What do you want me to say?" asked Hadley, in surprise.

"Well, never mind; it's your way, I suppose, and I can rely upon you."

"I should say so."

Mosely shrugged his shoulders. It was clearly idle to expect any great variety in Tom Hadley's conversation.

"Whatever we do must be done quickly," he said, in a quiet, decided tone. "They'll wake up before long, and there won't be any chance. You, Tom, take that near animal, and I'll tackle the other. Jest untie them quiet and easy, and when I say the word start. Do you understand?"

"I should say so, Bill," said Hadley, nodding.

"Then here goes."

In a few seconds they had loosened the mustangs and had sprung upon their backs.

"Now, go!" exclaimed Mosely, in a energetic whisper.

So on their stolen horses they drew stealthily away from the camp till they were perhaps a furlong away, and then, putting the mustangs to their speed, they soon put a distance of miles between them and their sleeping owners. They would have liked to remain long enough to have a trout breakfast, but that was impracticable.

CHAPTER XXVI.

WHAT NEXT?

Some persons are said to have premonitions of coming ill, but this could not be said in the present instance of Bradley and his young companion. Bradley had the shrewdness to read the real cowardice of Mosely, who was the leader, and did not dream that he would have the courage to take the horses. But then, he did not know the danger in which their two visitors had placed themselves by their recent theft. Danger will strengthen the courage of the timid, and, in this case, it decided Mosely to commit a new theft.

The robbers were quite five miles away when Ben opened his eyes.

He looked about him with sleepy eyes, and it was only by an effort that he remembered the events of the previous evening.

It was with no misgiving that he looked for the horses. When he realized that they were gone, his heart gave a great bound, and he rose on his elbow. Next he looked for Mosely and Hadley, but, of course, in vain.

"They've stolen the mustangs!" he said to himself, in genuine dismay, and instantly seizing Bradley by the shoulder, shook him energetically.

"What's the matter, Ben?" demanded Bradley, in amazement. "You needn't be quite so rough."

"It's time you were awake!" said Ben hurriedly. "Those fellows have stolen our mustangs!"

"What's that you say?" ejaculated Bradley, now thoroughly awake.

"The mustangs are gone, and they are gone!" said Ben.

"When did you find it out?"

"Only just now. I was sleepy, and overslept myself."

"Half-past seven o'clock," said Bradley, referring to a cheap silver watch which he had bought for a trifle from a miner at Murphy's who was hard up. "I'm afraid they must have been gone some time. It's a bad lookout for us, Ben."

"So it is, Jake. You thought they wouldn't dare to take anything."

"No more I thought they would. That Bill Mosely bragged so much I didn't think he had enough pluck."

"Does it take much pluck to be a thief, Jake?"

"Well, in Californy it does," answered Bradley. "When a man steals a boss here, he takes his life in his hand, and don't you forget it. If it was only a year in the penitentiary, or something like that, it wouldn't scare 'em so bad. That Mosely's a bad lot, and will likely die in his boots."

"What's that?"

"Be shot standing, or swing from the branch of a tree. I thought I'd said enough last night to put him off the notion of playin' us such a trick."

"Probably he thought there wouldn't be any chance of our catching him when we were reduced to walk."

"It's likely you're right, Ben, and I ought to have thought of that. I jest wish I could set eyes on the critter at this particular minute. To treat us that way after our kindness, that's what riles me."

"What shall we do, Jake?"

"That's to be considered. Blamed if I know, unless we foot it, and that will be no joke, over these hills and through these forests."

"We may come upon their track, and overtake them when they are not expecting it."

"I wish we might," said Bradley, the lines about his mouth tightening. "I'd give 'em a lesson."

"They are two men," said Ben thoughtfully, "and we are only a man and a boy."

"That is so, Ben; but I'll match you against Hadley. He don't amount to a row of pins; and if I can't tackle Bill Mosely, then I'll never show myself in 'Frisco again."

"I don't mind so much the loss of the mustangs," said Ben, "but I'm sorry that we shall be delayed in our search for Richard Dewey."

"That's bad, too. I expect that nice young lady in 'Frisco is a-waitin' anxiously to hear from him. Plague take that rascal Mosely!" he broke out, in fresh exasperation.

"Well, Jake, suppose we get some breakfast, and then consider what we will do."

"That's a good thought, Ben. We can't do much on an empty stomach, that's a fact."

For reasons which need not be specified, it was decided that the breakfast should consist of trout. Despite their loss, both had a good appetite, and when that was satisfied they became more hopeful.

CHAPTER XXVII.

KI SING.

Leaving Ben and his companion for a time, we go back to record an incident which will prove to have a bearing upon the fortunes of those in whom we are interested.

One morning two men, Taylor and O'Reilly, who had been out prospecting, came into camp, conveying between them, very much as two policemen conduct a prisoner, a terrifled-looking Chinaman, whose eyes, rolling helplessly from one to the other, seemed to indicate that he considered his position a very perilous one.

At that early period in the settlement of California, a few Chinamen had found their way to the Pacific coast; but the full tide of immigration did not set in till a considerable time later, and, therefore, the miners regarded one as a curiosity.

"Who have you got there, O'Reilly?" inquired one of his mining-comrades.

"A yeller haythen!" answered O'Eeilly. "Look at the craythur! Ain't he a beauty jist wid his long pigtail hangin' down his back like a monkey's tail?"

"Where did you find him?"

"He was huntin' for gold, the haythen, jist for all the world as if he was as white as you or I."

Mr. Patrick O'Reilly appeared to hold the opinion that gold-hunting should be confined to the Caucasian race. He looked upon a Chinaman as rather a superior order of monkey, suitable for exhibition in a cage, but not to be regarded as possessing the ordinary rights of an adopted American resident. If he could have looked forward twenty-five years, and foreseen the extent to which these barbarians would throng the avenues of employment, he would, no doubt, have been equally amazed and disgusted. Indeed, the capture of Ki Sing was made through his influence, as Taylor, a man from Ohio, was disposed to let him alone.

Soon a crowd gathered around the terrified Chinaman and his captors, and he was plied with questions, some of a jocular character, by the miners, who were glad of anything that relieved the monotony of their ordinary life.

"What's your name?" asked one.

The Chinaman gazed at the questioner vacantly.

"What's your name, you haythen?" repeated O'Reilly, emphasizing the inquiry by a powerful shake.

"My name Ki Sing," answered the Mongolian nervously.

"Where did you come from, old pigtail?"

"My name Ki Sing, not Pigtail," said the Chinaman, not understanding the meaning of the epithet.

This answer appeared to be regarded by the crowd as either witty or absurd, for it elicited a roar of laughter.

"Never mind what your name is, old stick in the mud! We'll call you whatever we please. Where do you come from?"

"Me come from 'Flisco."

It is well known that a Chinaman cannot pronounce the letter r, which in his mouth softens to l, in some cases producing a ludicrous effect.

"What have you come here for, Cy King, or whatever your name is."

"My name Ki Sing."

"Well, it's a haythen name; anyhow," remarked Mr. Patrick O'Eeilly. "Before I'd have such a name, I'd go widout one intirely. Did you hear the gintleman ask you what you came here for?"

"You bling me," answered Ki Sing shrewdly.

There was another laugh.

"That Chinee ain't no fool!" said Dick Roberts.

"What made you leave China?" he asked.

"Me come to Amelica fol gold."

"Hi, ho! That's it, is it? What are you going to do with your gold when you find it?"

"Cally it back to China."

"And when you've callied it back, what'll you do then?"

"Me mally wife, have good time and plenty money to buy lice."

Of course, Ki Sing's meaning was plain, but there was a roar of laughter, to which he listened with mild-eyed wonder, evidently thinking that the miners who so looked down on him were themselves a set of outside barbarians, to whom the superior civilization of China was utterly unknown. It is fortunate that his presumption was not suspected by those around him. No one would have resented it more than Mr. Patrick O'Reilly, whose rank as regards enlightenment and education certainly was not very high.

"I say, John," said Dick Roberts, "are you fond of rat pie?"

"Lat pie velly good," returned Ki Sing, with a look of appreciation.

"Melican man like him?"

"Hear the haythen!" said O'Reilly, with an expression of deep disgust. "He thinks we ate rats and mice, like him. No, old pigtail, we ain't cats. We are good Christians."

"Chlistian! Ma don't know Ghlistian," said the Chinaman.

"Then look at O'Reilly," said Dick Roberts, mischievously. "He's a good solid Christian."

Ki Sing turned his almond eyes upon O'Reilly, who, with his freckled face, wide mouth, broad nose, and stubby beard, was by no means a prepossessing-looking man, and said interrogatively: "He Chlistian?"

"Yes, John. Wouldn't you like to be one?"

Ki Sing shook his head decidedly.

"Me no want to be Chlistian," he answered. "Me velly well now. Me want to be good Chinaman."

"There's a compliment for you, O'Reilly," said one of the miners.

"John prefers to be a Chinaman to being like you."

"He's a barbarious haythen, anyhow," said O'Reilly, surveying his prisoner with unfriendly eyes. "What did he come over to America for, anyhow?"

"He probably came over for the same reason that brought you, O'Reilly," said a young man, who spoke for the first time, though he had been from the outset a disgusted witness of what had taken place.

"And what's that?" demanded O'Reilly angrily.

"To make a living," answered Richard Dewey quietly.

As this is the first time this young man has been introduced, we will briefly describe him. He was of medium size, well knit and vigorous, with a broad forehead, blue eyes, and an intelligent and winning countenance. He might have been suspected of too great amiability and gentleness, but for a firm expression about the mouth, and an indefinable air of manliness, which indicated that it would not do to go too far with him. There was a point, as all his friends knew, where his forbearance gave way and he sternly asserted his rights. He was not so popular in camp as some, because he declined to drink or gamble, and, despite the rough circumstances in which he found himself placed, was resolved to preserve his self-respect.

O'Reilly did not fancy his interference, and demanded, in a surly tone:

"Do you mean to compare me wid this haythen?"

"You are alike in one respect," said Richard Dewey quietly. "Neither of you were born in this country, but each of you came here to improve your fortunes."

"And hadn't I the right, I'd like to know?" blustered O'Reilly.

"To be sure you had. This country is free to all who wish to make a home here."

"Then what are you talkin' about, anyway?"

"You ought to be able to understand without asking. Ki Sing has come here, and has the same right that you have."

"Do you mane to put me on a livel wid him?"

"In that one respect, I do."

"I want you to understand that Patrick O'Reilly won't take no insults from you, nor any other man!"

"Hush, O'Reilly!" said Terence O'Gorman, another Irish miner. "Dewey is perfectly right. I came over from Ireland like you, but he hasn't said anything against either of us."

"That is where you are right, O'Gorman," said Richard Dewey cordially. "You are a man of sense, and can understand me. My own father emigrated from England, and I am not likely to say anything against the class to which he belonged. Now, boys, you have had enough sport out of the poor Chinaman. I advise you to let him go."

Ki Sing grasped at this suggestion.

"Melican man speak velly good," he said.

"Of course, you think so," sneered O'Reilly. "I say, boys, let's cut off his pigtail," touching the poor Chinaman's queue.

Ki Sing uttered a cry of dismay as O'Reilly's suggestion was greeted with favorable shouts by the thoughtless crowd.

CHAPTER XXVIII.
THE DUEL OF THE MINERS.

O'Reilly's suggestion chimed in with the rough humor of the crowd. They were not bad-hearted men, but, though rough in their manners, not much worse on the average than an equal number of men in the Eastern States. They only thought of the fun to be obtained from the proceeding, and supposed they would be doing the Chinaman no real harm.

"Has anybody got a pair of scissors?" asked O'Reilly, taking the

Chinaman by the queue.

"I've got one in my tent," answered one of the miners.

"Go and get it, then."

Ki Sing again uttered a cry of dismay, but it did not seem likely that his valued appendage could be saved. Public sentiment was with his persecutor.

He had one friend, however, among the rough men who surrounded him, the same who had already taken his part.

Richard Dewey's eyes glittered sternly as he saw O'Reilly's intention, and he quietly advanced till he was within an arm's length of Ki Sing.

"What do you mean to do, O'Reilly?" he demanded sternly.

"None of your business!" retorted O'Reilly insolently.

"It is going to be my business. What do you mean to do?"

"Gut off this haythen's pigtail, and I'd just like to know who's going to prevent me."

At this moment the miner who had gone for a pair of scissors returned.

"Give me them scissors!" said O'Reilly sharply.

Richard Dewey reached out his hand and intercepted them. He took them in place of O'Reilly.

"Give me them scissors, Dewey, or it'll be the worse for you!" exclaimed the tyrant furiously.

Dewey regarded him with a look of unmistakable contempt.

There was a murmur among the miners, who were eager for the amusement which the Chinaman's terror and ineffectual struggles would afford them.

"Give him the scissors, Dewey!" said half a dozen.

"Boys," said Dewey, making no motion to obey them, "do you know what you are about to do? Why should you interfere with this poor, unoffending Chinaman? Has he wronged any one of you?"

"No, but that ain't the point," said a Kentuckian. "We only want to play a joke on him. It won't do him no harm to cut his hair."

"Of course not," chimed in several of the miners.

"Do you hear that, Dick Dewey?" demanded O'Reilly impatiently. "Do you hear what the boys say? Give me them scissors."

"Boys, you don't understand the effects of what you would do," said Dewey, taking no notice of O'Reilly, much to that worthy's indignation. "If Ki Sing has his queue cut off, he can never go back to China."

"Is that the law, squire?" asked a loose-jointed Yankee.

"Yes, it is. You may rely on my word. Ki Sing, if you cut off your queue, can you go back to China?"

"No go back-stay in Melica allee time."

"You see he confirms my statement."

"That's a queer law, anyway," said the Kentuckian.

"I admit that, but such as it is, we can't alter it. Now, Ki Sing has probably a father and mother, perhaps a wife and children, in China. He wants to go back to them some time. Shall we prevent this, and doom him to perpetual exile, just to secure a little sport? Come, boys, you've all of you got dear ones at home, that you hope some day to see again. I appeal to you whether this is manly or kind."

This was a sort of argument that had a strong effect. It was true that each one of these men had relatives for whom they were working, the thought of whom enabled them to bear hard work and privations thousands of miles away from home, and Richard Dewey's appeal touched their hearts.

"That's so! Dewey is right. Let him go, O'Reilly!" said the crowd.

The one man who was not touched by the appeal was O'Reilly himself. Not that he was altogether a bad man, but his spirit of opposition was kindled, and he could not bear to yield to Dewey, whose contempt he understood and resented.

His reply was, "I'm goin' to cut off the haythen's pigtail, whether or no. Give me them scissors, I tell you," and he gave a vicious twitch to the Chinaman's queue, which made Ki Sing utter a sharp cry of pain.

Richard Dewey's forbearance was at an end. His eyes blazed with fury, and, clenching his fist, he dashed it full in the face of the offending O'Reilly, who not only released his hold on Ki Sing, but measured his length on the ground.

O'Reilly was no coward, and he possessed the national love of a shindy. He sprang to his feet in a rage, and shouted:

"I'll murder ye for that, Dick Dewey! See if I don't!"

"A fight! a fight!" shouted the miners, willing to be amused in that way, since they had voluntarily given up the fun expected from cutting off the Chipaman's queue.

Richard Dewey looked rather disgusted.

"I don't want to fight, boys," he said. "It isn't to my taste."

"You've got to, you coward!" said O'Reilly, beginning to bluster.

"I don't think you'll find me a coward," said Dewey quietly, as he stood with his arms folded, looking at O'Reilly.

"You'll have to give O'Reilly satisfaction," said one of the miners.

"You've knocked him down, and he's got a right to it."

"Will it be any satisfaction to him to get knocked over again?" asked

Dewey, shrugging his shoulders.

"You can't do it! I'll bate you till you can't stand!" exclaimed the angry Irishman. "I'll tache you to insult a gintleman."

"Form a ring, boys!" exclaimed the Kentuck-ian. "We'll see there's fair play."

"One thing first," said Dewey, holding up his hand. "If I come off best in this encounter, you'll all agree to let this Chinaman go free? Is that agreed?"

"Yes, yes, it is agreed!"

Ki Sing stood trembling with fear while these preliminaries were being settled. He would have escaped from the crowd, but his first movement was checked.

"No, Cy King, we can't let you go jest yet," said Taylor. "We're goin' to see this thing through first."

O'Reilly was not in the least daunted by the contest in which he was to engage. Indeed, he felt a good deal of satisfaction at the prospect of being engaged in a scrimmage. Of course, he expected to come off a victor. He was a considerably larger man than Richard Dewey, with arms like flails and flats like sledge-hammers, and he had no sort of doubt that he could settle his smaller antagonist in less than five minutes.

But there was one thing of which he was not aware. Though slender, Dewey had trained and hardened his muscles by exercise in a gymnasium, and, moreover, he had taken a course of lessons in the manly art of self-defense. He had done this, not because he expected to be called upon to defend himself at any time, but because he thought it conducive to keeping up his health and strength. He awaited O'Reilly's onset with watchful calmness.

O'Reilly advanced with a whoop, flinging about his powerful arms somewhat like a windmill, and prepared to upset his antagonist at the first onset.

What was his surprise to find his own blows neatly parried, and to meet a tremendous blow from his opponent which set his nose to bleeding.

Astonished, but not panic-stricken, he pluckily advanced to a second round, and tried to grasp Dewey round the waist. But instead of doing this, he received another knock-down blow, which stretched him on the ground.

He was up again, and renewed the attack, but with even less chance of victory than before, for the blood was streaming down his face, and he could not see distinctly where to hit. Dewey contented himself with keeping on guard and parrying the blows of his demoralized adversary.

"It's no use, O'Reilly!" exclaimed two or three. "Dewey's the better man."

"Let me get at him! I'll show him what I can do," said O'Reilly doggedly.

"As long as you like, O'Reilly," said Richard Dewey coolly; "but you may as well give it up."

"Troth and I won't. I'm stronger than you are any day."

"Perhaps you are; but I understand fighting, and you don't."

"An O'Reilly not know how to fight!" exclaimed the Irishman hotly.

"I could fight when I was six years old."

"Perhaps so; but you can't box."

One or two more attacks, and O'Reilly was dragged away by two of his friends, and Dewey remained master of the field.

The miners came up and shook hands with him cordially. They regarded him with new respect, now that it was found he had overpowered the powerful O'Reilly.

Among those who congratulated him was his Mongolian friend, Ki Sing.

"Melican man good fightee-knock over Ilishman. Hullah!"

"Come with me, Ki Sing," said Dewey. "'I will take care of you till to-morrow, and then you had better go."

CHAPTER XXIX.

CHINESE CHEAP LABOR.

Though Dewey had received from the miners a promise that they would not interfere with Ki Sing in case he gained a victory over O'Reilly, he was not willing to trust entirely to it. He feared that some one would take it into his head to play a trick on the unoffending Chinaman, and that the others unthinkingly would join in. Accordingly, he thought it best to keep the Mongolian under his personal charge as long as he remained in camp.

Ki Sing followed him to his tent as a child follows a guardian.

"Are you hungry, Ki Sing?" asked Dewey.

"Plenty hungly."

"Then I will first satisfy your appetite," and Dewey brought forth some of his stock of provisions, to which Ki Sing did ample justice, though neither rat pie nor rice was included.

When the lunch, in which Richard Dewey joined, was over, he said: "If you will help me for the rest of the day, I will pay you whatever I consider your services to be worth."

"All lightee!" responded Ki Sing, with alacrity.

Whatever objections may be made to the Chinaman, he cannot be charged with laziness. As a class they are willing to labor faithfully, even where the compensation is small. Labor in China, which is densely peopled, is a matter of general and imperative necessity, and has been so for centuries, and habit has probably had a good deal to do with the national spirit of industry.

Ki Sing, under Richard Dewey's directions, worked hard, and richly earned the two dollars which his employer gave him at the end of the day.

Of course Dewey's action did not escape the attention of his fellow miners. It cannot be said that they regarded it with favor. The one most offended was naturally O'Reilly, who, despite the pounding he had received, was about the camp as usual.

"Boys," he said, "are you goin' to have that haythen workin' alongside you?"

"It won't do us any harm, will it?" asked Dick Roberts. "If Dewey chooses to hire him, what is it to us?"

"I ain't goin' to demane myself by workin' wid a yeller haythen."

"Nobody has asked you to do it. If anybody is demeaning himself it is Dick Dewey, and he has a right to if he wants to."

"If he wants to hire anybody, let him hire a dacent Christian."

"Like you, O'Reilly?"

"I don't want to work for anybody. I work for myself. This Chinaman has come here to take the bread out of our mouths, bad cess to him."

"I don't see that. He is workin' Dick Dewey's claim. I don't see how that interferes with us."

Of course, this was the reasonable view of the matter; but there were some who sided with the Irishman, among others the Kentuckian, and he volunteered to go as a committee of one to Dewey, and represent to him the sentiments of the camp.

Accordingly he walked over to where Dewey and his apprentice were working.

"Look here, Dewey," he began, "me and some of the rest of the boys have takin' over this yere matter of your givin' work to this Chinaman, and we don't like it."

"Why not?" asked Dewey coolly.

"We don't feel no call to associate with sich as he."

"You needn't; I don't ask you to," said Dewey quietly. "I am the only one who associates with him."

"But we don't want him in camp."

"He won't trouble any of you. I will take charge of him."

"Look here, Dewey, you've got to respect public sentiment, and public sentiment is agin' this thing."

"Whose public sentiment—O'Reilly's?"

"Well, O'Reilly don't like it, for one."

"I thought so."

"Nor I for another."

"It strikes me, Hodgson, that I've got some rights as well as O'Reilly. Suppose I should say I didn't choose to work in the same camp with an Irishman?"

"That's different."

"Why is it different?"

"Well, you see, an Irishman isn't a yeller heathen."

Dewey laughed.

"He may be a heathen, though not a yellow one," he said.

"Well, Dewey, what answer shall I take back to the boys?"

"You can say that I never intended to employ the Chinaman for any length of time; but I shall not send him off till I get ready."

"I'm afraid the boys won't like it, Dewey."

"Probably O'Reilly won't. As for you, you are too intelligent a man to be influenced by such a man as he."

All men are sensible to flattery, and Hodgson was won over by this politic speech.

"I won't say you're altogether wrong, Dewey," he said; "but I wouldn't keep him too long."

"I don't mean to."

Hodgson returning reported that Dewey would soon dismiss the Chinaman, and omitted the independent tone which the latter had assumed. The message was considered conciliatory, and pronounced satisfactory; but O'Reilly was not appeased. He still murmured, but his words produced little effect. Seeing this, he devised a private scheme of annoyance.

CHAPTER XXX.

A MIDNIGHT VISIT.

This conversation set Dewey to thinking. Though he was independent, he was not foolishly so, and he was not willing, out of a spirit of opposition, to expose his new acquaintance to annoyance, perhaps to injury. He did not care to retain Ki Sing in his employment for any length of time, and made up his mind to dismiss him early the next mornng, say, at four o'clock, before the miners had thrown off the chains of sleep.

He did not anticipate any harm to his Mongolian friend during the night; but this was because he did not fully understand the feeling of outraged dignity which rankled in the soul of O'Reilly.

Patrick O'Reilly was like his countrymen in being always ready for a fight; but he was unlike them in harboring a sullen love of revenge. In this respect he was more like an Indian.

He felt that Richard Dewey had got the better of him in the brief contest, and the fact that he had been worsted in the presence of his fellow miners humiliated him. If he could only carry his point, and deprive the Chinaman of his queue after all, the disgrace would be redeemed, and O'Reilly would be himself again.

"And why shouldn't I?" he said to himself. "The haythen will sleep in Dewey's tent. Why can't I creep up, unbeknownst, in the middle of the night, and cut off his pigtail, while he is aslape? Faith, I'd like to see how he and his friend would look in the morning. I don't belave a word of his not bein' allowed to go back to Chiny widout it. That is an invintion of Dewey."

The more O'Reilly dwelt upon this idea the more it pleased him. Once the pigtail was cut off, the mischief could not be repaired, and he would have a most suitable and satisfactory revenge.

Of course, it would not do to make the attempt till Ki Sing and his protector were both fast asleep. "All men are children when they are asleep," says an old proverb. That is, all men are as helpless as children when their senses are locked in slumber. It would be safer, therefore, to carry out his plan if he could manage to do so without awaking the two men.

O'Reilly determined not to take any one into his confidence. This was prudent, for it was sure to prevent his plan from becoming known. There was, however, one inconvenience about this, as it would prevent him from borrowing the scissors upon which he had relied to cut off the queue. But he had a sharp knife, which he thought would answer the purpose equally well.

It was rather hard for O'Reilly to keep awake till midnight-the earliest hour which he thought prudent-but the motive which impelled him was sufficiently strong to induce even this sacrifice.

So, as the shadows darkened, and the night came on, Patrick O'Reilly forced himself to lie awake, while he waited eagerly for the hour of midnight. Meanwhile, Richard Dewey and Ki Sing lay down at nine o'clock and sought refreshment in sleep. Both were fatigued, but it was the Chinaman who first lost consciousness. Dewey scanned with curiosity the bland face of his guest, looking childlike and peaceful, as he lay by his side.

"I wonder if he is dreaming of his distant home in China," thought Dewey. "The cares of life do not seem to sit heavy upon him. Though he has been in danger to-day, and may be so still, he yields himself up trustfully to the repose which he needs. Is it true, I wonder, that cares increase with mental culture? Doubtless, it is true. If I were in China, threatened with a loss which would prevent my returning to my native country, I am sure it would keep me awake. But there can be nothing to fear now."

Richard raised himself on his elbow, and looked about him. The tents of the miners were grouped together, within a comparatively small radius, and on all sides could be heard-it was now past ten-the deep breathing of men exhausted by the day's toils. This would not ordinarily have been the case at so early an hour, for when there was whisky in the camp, there was often late carousing. It chanced, however, at this time that the stock of liquor was exhausted, and, until a new supply could be obtained from San Francisco, necessity enforced the rule of total abstinence. It would have been well if, for months to come, there could have been the same good reason for abstinence, but, as a matter of fact, the very next day some casks were brought into camp, much to the delighted and satisfaction of the anti-temperance party.

Finally Dewey fell asleep, but his sleep was a troubled one. He had unthinkingly reclined upon his back, and this generally brought bad dreams. He woke with a start from a dream, in which it seemed to him that the miners were about to hang Ki Sing from the branch of one of the tall trees near-by, when he detected a stealthy step close at hand.

Instantly he was on the alert. Turning his head, he caught sight of a human figure nearing the tent. A second glance showed him that it was O'Reilly, with a knife in his hand.

"Good heavens!" thought Dewey, "does he mean to kill the poor

Chinaman?"

A muttered sentence from O'Reilly reassured him on this point.

"Now, you yeller haythen, I'll cut off your pigtail in spite of that impertinent friend of yours—Dick Dewey. I'll show you that an O'Reilly isn't to be interfered wid."

"So he wants the poor fellow's queue, does he?" said Dewey to himself. "You're not quite smart enough, Mr. O'Reilly."

There was no time to lose.

O'Reilly was already on his knees, with the poor Chinaman's treasured queue in his hand, when he felt himself seized in a powerful grip.

"What are you about, O'Reilly?" demanded Richard Dewey, in a deep, stern voice.

O'Reilly uttered a cry, rather of surprise than alarm.

"What are you about?" repeated Richard Dewey, in a tone of authority.

"I'm goin' to cut off the haythen's pigtail," answered the Irishman doggedly.

"What for?"

"I've said I'd do it, and I'll do it."

"Well, Mr. O'Reilly, I've said you sha'n't do it, and I mean to keep my word."

O'Reilly tried to carry out his intent, but suddenly found himself flung backward in a position very favorable for studying the position of the stars.

"Are you not ashamed to creep up to my tent in the middle of the night on such an errand as that, Patrick O'Reilly?" demanded Dewey.

"No, I'm not. Let me up, Dick Dewey, or it'll be the worse for you," said the intruder wrathfully.

"Give me your knife, then."

"I won't. It's my own."

"The errand on which you come is my warrant for demanding it."

"I won't give you the knife, but I'll go back," said O'Reilly.

"That won't do."

"Don't you go too far, Dick Dewey. I'm your aiqual."

"No man is my equal who creeps to my tent at the dead of night. Do you know what the camp will think, O'Eeilly?"

"And what will they think?"

"That you came to rob me."

"Then they'll think a lie!" said O'Reilly, startled, for he knew that on such a charge he would be liable to be suspended to the nearest tree.

"If they chose to think so, it would be bad for you."

"You know it isn't so Dick Dewey," said O'Reilly.

"I consider your intention quite as bad. You wanted to prevent this poor Chinaman from ever returning to his native land, though he had never injured you in any way. You can't deny it."

"I don't belave a word of all that rigmarole, Dick Dewey."

"It makes little difference whether you believe it or not. You have shown a disposition to injure and annoy Ki Sing, but I have foiled you. And now," here

Dewey's tone became deep and stern, "give me that knife directly, and go back to your tent, or I'll rouse the camp, and they may form their own conclusions as to what brought you here."

O'Reilly felt that Dewey was in earnest, and that he must yield. He did so with a bad grace enough and slunk back to his tent, which he did not leave till morning.

Early in the morning, Richard Dewey awakened Ki Sing.

"You had better not stay here, Ki Sing," he said. "There are those who would do you mischief. Go into the mountains, and you may find gold. There you will be safe."

"Melican man velly good-me go," said the Chinaman submissively.

"Good luck to you, Ki Sing!"

"Good luckee, Melican man!"

So the two parted, and when morning came to the camp, nothing was to be seen of the Chinaman.

Dewey returned O'Reilly's knife, the latter receiving it in sullen silence.

It was not long afterward that Richard Dewey himself left Murphy's in search of a richer claim.

CHAPTER XXXI.

ON THE MOUNTAIN PATH.

My readers will not have forgotten Bill Mosely and his companion Tom Hadley, who played the mean trick upon Bradley and our hero of stealing their horses. I should be glad to state that they were overtaken and punished within twenty-four hours, but it would not be correct. They had a great advantage over their pursuers, who had only their own feet to help them on, and, at the end of the first day, were at least ten miles farther on than Ben and Bradley.

As the two last, wearied and well-nigh exhausted, sat down to rest,

Bradley glanced about him long and carefully in all directions.

"I can't see anything of them skunks, Ben," he said.

"I suppose not, Jake. They must be a good deal farther on."

"Yes, I reckon so. They've got the horses to help them, while we've got to foot it. It was an awful mean trick they played on us."

"That's so, Jake."

"All I ask is to come up with 'em some of these days."

"What would you do?"

"I wouldn't take their lives, for I ain't no murderer, but I'd tie 'em hand and foot, and give 'em a taste of a horsewhip, or a switch, till they'd think they was schoolboys again."

"You might not be able to do it. They would be two to one."

"Not quite, Ben. I'd look for some help from you."

"I would give you all the help I could," said Ben.

"I know you mean it, and that you wouldn't get scared, and desert me, as a cousin of mine did once when I was set upon by robbers."

"Was that in California?"

"No; in Kentucky. I had a tough job, but I managed to disable one of the rascals, and the other ran away."

"What did your cousin have to say?"

"He told me, when I caught up with him, that he was goin' in search of help, but I told him that was too thin. I told him I wouldn't keep his company any longer, and that he had better go his way and I would go mine. He tried to explain things, but there are some things that ain't so easily explained, that I wouldn't hear him. I stick to my friends, and I expect them to stand by me."

"That's fair, Jake."

"That's the way I look at it. I wonder where them rascals are?"

"You mean Mosely and his friend?"

"Yes. What galls me, Ben, is that they're likely laughin' in their shoes at the way they've tricked us, and there's no help for it."

"Not just now, Jake, but we may overtake them yet. Till we do, we may as well take things as easy as we can."

"You're right, Ben. You'mind me of an old man that used to live in the place where I was raised. He never borrered any trouble, but when things was contrary, he waited for 'em to take a turn. When he saw a neighbor frettin', he used to say, 'Fret not thy gizzard, for it won't do no good.'"

Ben laughed.

"That was good advice," he said.

"I don't know where he got them words from. Maybe they're in the

Bible."

"I guess not," said Ben, smiling. "They don't sound like it."

"Perhaps you're right," said Bradley, not fully convinced, however. "Seems to me I've heard old Parson Brown get off something to that effect."

"Perhaps it was this-'Sufficient unto the day is the evil thereof.'"

"Perhaps it was. Is that from the Bible?"

"Yes."

"It might have been made a little stronger," said Bradley thoughtfully. "The evil of some days is more than sufficient, accordin' to my notion."

The two explorers camped out as usual, and the fatigue of their day's tramp insured them a deep, refreshing sleep. The next day they resumed their journey, and for several days to come no incident worthy of mention varied the monotony of their march. Toward the close of the fourth day they saw from a distance a figure approaching them, who seemed desirous of attracting their attention. Ben was the first to see him.

"Jake," said he, "look yonder!"

"It's a Chinee!" said Bradley, in surprise.

"How did the critter come here, in the name of wonder?"

"I suppose he is looking for gold as well as we."

"The heathen seems to be signalin' us. He's wavin' his arm."

This was the case. The Chinaman, for some reason, seemed to wish to attract the attention of the newcomers. He stopped short, and waited for Ben and Bradley to come up.

"Who are you, my yeller friend?" asked Bradley, when he was near enough to be heard.

"My name Ki Sing."

"Glad to hear it. I can't say I ever heard of your family, but I reckon from the name, it's a musical one."

Ki Sing probably did not understand the tenor of Bradley's remark.

"Is there any hotel round here, Mr. Sing?" asked Ben jocosely, "where two weary travelers can put up for the night?"

"Nohotellee!"

"Then where do you sleep?"

"Me sleep on glound."

"Your bed is a pretty large one, then," said Bradley. "The great objection to it is, that it is rather hard."

Ki Sing's mind was evidently occupied by some engrossing thought, which prevented his paying much attention to Bradley's jocose observations.

"Melican man wantee you," he said, in an excited manner.

"What's that?" asked Bradley. "Melican man want me?"

Ki Sing nodded.

"Where is he?"

Ki Sing turned, and pointed to a rude hut some half a mile away in a little mountain nook.

"Melican man thele," he said.

"Come along, Ben," said Bradley. "Let us see what this means. It may be some countryman of ours who is in need of help."

The Chinaman trotted along in advance, and our two friends followed him.

CHAPTER XXXII.

THE MOUNTAIN CABIN.

At length they reached the entrance to the cabin. It was a rough structure, built of logs, containing but one apartment. On a blanket in one corner of the hut lay a young man, looking pale and emaciated. His face was turned to the wall, so that, though he heard steps, he did not see who crossed the threshold.

"Is that you, Ki Sing?" he asked, in a low voice. "But why need I ask? There is not likely to be any one else in this lonely spot."

"That's where you're mistaken, my friend," said Bradley. "I met that Chinaman of yours half a mile away, and he brought me here. You're sick, I reckon?"

The invalid started in surprise and evident joy when he heard

Bradley's voice.

"Thank Heaven!" he said, "for the sound of a countryman's voice," and he turned to look at his visitor.

Now it was Bradley's turn to start and manifest surprise.

"Why, it's Dick Dewey!" he exclaimed.

"You know me?" said the sick man eagerly.

"Of course I do. Didn't we work together at Murphy's, almost side by side?"

"Jake Bradley!" exclaimed Dewey, recognizing him at last.

"The same old coon! Now, Dewey, what's the matter with you?"

"Nothing serious, but enough to lay me up for a time. A week since I slipped from a rock and sprained my ankle severely-so much so that I can't use it safely. I've often heard that a sprain is worse than a break, but I never realized it till now."

"Has the Chinaman taken care of you?" inquired Bradley.

"Yes; I don't know what I should have done without Ki Sing," said

Dewey, with a grateful glance at the Chinaman.

"Was he with you when the accident hapened?"

"No; I lay helpless on the hillside for two hours, when, providentially, as I shall always consider it, my friend Ki Sing came along."

The Chinaman usually impassive face seemed to light up with pleasure when Richard Dewey spoke of him as his friend.

"I tell you what, Ki Sing," said Bradley, turning to the representative of China, "I never thought much of your people before, but I cheerfully admit that you're a brick."

"A blick!" repeated the Mongolian, appearing more puzzled than complimented.

"Yes, a brick-a real good fellow, and no mistake! Give us your hand!

You're a gentleman!"

Ki Sing readily yielded his hand to the grasp of the miner. He saw that Bradley meant to be friendly, though he did not altogether understand him.

"Had you ever met Ki Sing, Dick?" asked Bradley.

"Yes; on one occasion I had a chance to be of service to him, and he had not forgotten it. He has taken the best care of me, and supplied me with food, which I was unable to procure for myself. I think I should have starved but for him."

"Ki Sing, I want to shake hands with you again," said Bradley, who seemed a good deal impressed by conduct which his prejudices would not have allowed him to expect from a heathen.

Ki Sing winced beneath the strong pressure of the miner's grasp, and examined his long, slender fingers with some anxiety when he rescued them from the cordial, but rather uncomfortable pressure.

"Melican man shakee too much!" he protested.

Bradley did not hear him, for he had again resumed conversation with

Dewey.

"Is that your boy, Bradley?" asked the invalid, glaring at Ben, who modestly kept in the background.

"No, it's a young friend of mine that I came across in 'Frisco. His name is Ben Stanton. I don't believe you can guess what brought us up here among the mountains."

"Probably you came, like me, in search of gold."

"That's where you're wrong. Leastways, that wasn't the principal object of our coming."

"You're not traveling for pleasure, I should think," said Dewey, smiling.

"Not much. Since our hosses have been stole, there's mighty little pleasure in clamberin' round on these hills. The fact is, we've been lookin' for you."

"Looking for me!" exclaimed Dewey, in great surprise.

"Yes, and no mistake. Isn't it so, Ben?"

Ben nodded assent.

"But what possible motive can you have in looking for me?"

"I say, Dewey," proceeded Bradley, "did you ever hear of a young lady by the name of Florence Douglas?"

The effect of the name was electric. Dewey sprang up in bed, and inquired eagerly.

"Yes, yes, but what of her? Can you tell me anything of her?"

"I can tell you as much as this: she is in 'Frisco, and has sent out

Ben and me to hunt you up, and let you know where she is."

"Is this true? How came she here? Is her guardian with her?" asked

Dewey rapidly.

"One question at a time, Dick. The fact is, she's given her guardian the slip, and came out to Californy in charge of my young friend, Ben. I hope you won't be jealous of him."

"If she trusts him, I will also," said Dewey. "Tell me the whole story, my lad. If you have been her friend, you may depend on my gratitude."

Ben told the story clearly and intelligibly, replying also to such questions as Richard Dewey was impelled to ask him, and his straightforwardness produced a very favorable impression on his new acquaintance.

"I begin to see, that, young as you are, Florence didn't make a bad selection when she chose you as her escort."

"Now, Dewey," said Bradley, "I've got some advice to give you. Get well as soon as you can, and go to 'Frisco yourself. I surmise Miss Douglas won't need Ben any longer when you are with her."

"You forget this confounded sprain," said Dewey, looking ruefully at his ankle. "If I go you'll have to carry me."

"Then get well as soon as you can. We'll stay with you till you're ready. If there was only a claim round here that Ben and I could work while we are waitin', it would make the time pass pleasanter."

"There is," said Dewey. "A month since I made a very valuable discovery, and had got out nearly a thousand dollars' worth of gold, when I was taken down. You two are welcome to work it, for as soon as I am in condition, I shall go back to San Francisco."

"We'll give you a share of what we find, Dick."

"No, you won't. The news you have brought me is worth the claim many times over. I shall give Ki Sing half of what I have in the cabin here as a recompense for his faithful service."

Ki Sing looked well content, as he heard this promise, and his smile became even more "childlike and bland" than usual, as he bustled about to prepare the evening meal.

"I'll tell you what, Ben," said Bradley, "we'll pay Ki Sing something besides, and he shall be our cook and steward, and see that we have three square meals a day."

"I agree to that," said Ben.

When Ki Sing was made to comprehend the proposal, he, too, agreed, and the little household was organized. The next day Ben and Bradley went to work at Dewey's claim, which they found unexpectedly rich, while the Chinaman undertook the duties assigned him. Four weeks elapsed before Richard Dewey was in a condition to leave the cabin for San Francisco. Then he and Ben returned, Ki Sing accompanying them as a servant, while Bradley remained behind to guard Dewey's claim and work it during Ben's absence.

THE END.

www.ingramcontent.com/pod-product-compliance
Lightning Source LLC
Chambersburg PA
CBHW080909190726
48294CB00008B/2023